FOREVER WILD

ALSO BY K.A. TUCKER

Ten Tiny Breaths

One Tiny Lie

Four Seconds to Lose

Five Ways to Fall

In Her Wake

Burying Water

Becoming Rain

Chasing River

Surviving Ice

He Will Be My Ruin

Until It Fades

Keep Her Safe

The Simple Wild

Be the Girl

Say You Still Love Me

Wild at Heart

The Player Next Door

FOREVER WILD

a novella

K.A. TUCKER

This book is a work of fiction. Any references to historical events, real people, or real places are used fictitiously. Other names, characters, places, and events are products of the author's imagination, and any resemblance to actual events or places or persons, living or dead, is entirely coincidental.

ISBN 978-1-7772027-2-9

ISBN 978-1-7772027-4-3 (ebook)

Edited by Jennifer Sommersby

Cover design by Hang Le

Published by K.A.Tucker

Manufactured in the United States of America

To everyone who has fallen in love with Calla and Jonah.

CHAPTER ONE

December

"She out there again?"

"Somewhere. Those are fresh tracks." The mama moose hasn't been seen much around here in the last few months. I assume because of a certain wolf dog that has made a second home of our property. But she's been coming around again lately. I've watched her nibble on frozen branches every morning this week, unaware—or more likely unperturbed—by my looming presence at the bay window. I've even managed to snap a few photos to stock my Alaska-centric Instagram feed.

I sip my latte, savoring the warmth that flows down my throat as I admire the vast frozen expanse. A fresh coat of snow fell overnight, for the fourth night in a row, blanketing our little haven just outside the small town of Trapper's Crossing in white.

"I probably scared her away with the plow." Jonah leans in to press a morning kiss against my neck, his scruffy beard tickling my skin.

My nose catches the scent of woodsy soap, and I inhale

deeply. In the weeks leading up to the busy holiday season, this has become one of my favorite parts of the day. The quiet calm before the flurry of daily tasks, when there's nothing but the sound of crackling logs in the hearth and I have a few moments of Jonah's undivided attention. We'll both be running soon enough. Or flying, in Jonah's case.

I close my eyes and dip my head to the side, to give him better access. "You were up early this morning."

"It got cold last night. Wanted to make sure everything was running all right."

Jonah was up early because he was tossing and turning all night, *again*. I know it has nothing to do with the frigid temperature and everything to do with his mother and stepfather's arrival from Oslo today. While he's excited to see Astrid, the same can't be said for Björn.

"Everything will be *fine,*" I promise for the umpteenth time, reaching up to smooth my palm across his cheek. I nod at the small cabin peeking out from the trees on the opposite side of our private lake. "They'll be *all the way* over *there,* sleeping off twenty hours of travel for the next couple days. By the time they wake up, my mom and Simon will be here." Exhilaration flares in my chest. It's been almost a year to the day since they dropped me off at the airport with a one-way ticket to my new life in Alaska. A lifetime ago, it seems. "And then Agnes and Mabel will be here on *Monday*. There's plenty of buffer between you and Björn."

"A buffer isn't going to stop him from treating my mother like a damn servant," he mutters.

Aside from the long list of grievances Jonah has with his stepfather, including general laziness and incessant complaining and nitpicking, his biggest issue with Björn is the expectation he has set for Astrid, to cook and clean and keep the house in order. This is his second marriage, and their civil ceremony happened just three weeks after the divorce from his first wife was finalized

—according to Jonah, his stepfather can't survive being single. He couldn't find his way around a kitchen if his life depended on it.

If half of what Jonah has told me is true, I'm not thrilled to be spending two weeks with the chauvinistic, old-fashioned ass, either, but I won't feed Jonah's anxiety by admitting that.

"I promise, this Christmas will be *perfect*."

Jonah's derisive snort says otherwise, but I sense the tension in his body relaxing a touch.

"Well, *I*'m excited. It's our first Christmas in this house. And, I mean, *look* at it." I've spent the last month mining for creative holiday ideas, foraging for supplies, and burning my fingers with hot glue late into the night. From the twelve-foot spruce that Jonah cut and dragged in from the woods, to the mammoth fieldstone fireplace adorned with an evergreen wreath and surrounded by old-timey lanterns, to the inviting reading nook beneath the stairs, decorated in buffalo plaid cushions and blankets, our home is dressed to the nines for the festivities.

The rustic house that we strolled into last March, cluttered with dead animals, shabby furnishings, and the remnants of a thirty-year marriage, has given way to a cozy, chic log home that I'm proud of, that we're about to welcome our families into for the first time. Even Muriel declared it belongs in "one of those overpriced magazines." Literally, the only thing it's missing to be the perfect Christmas home is a mantel. I've hung our stockings off hooks on the windowsill for the time being.

More important than how it looks is that it's a home I now long to return to each day.

But not nearly as much as I long to return to this man cradling me in his arms each night.

"Told you that $3000 antler chandelier was perfect for this room," Jonah quips.

My glare earns his boisterous laughter.

"You did good, Barbie." He steals a quick kiss. "Okay, gotta go. Too much shit to do before I head to the airport. Rick's probably already waiting for me." Rick, the scout who has paid The Yeti a large sum to tour frozen Alaska the past week, looking for ideal filming locations.

While I'm happy Jonah has had steady work through our little charter company since his arm healed, a part in my stomach clenches every time he flies. "You filled out an itinerary, right?"

"It's on your desk."

"Stick to it." My voice takes on a now-familiar warning tone. While Jonah's been much better about keeping schedules and calling in, he still gets caught up sometimes and forgets.

"Yeah, boss." He gives my backside a firm squeeze before marching for the front door.

"That's workplace harassment!" I holler after him.

He pauses to offer a sly smile over his shoulder. "And what do you call what you did to me in the office yesterday?"

"Your Christmas bonus."

His deep, grating chuckle warms my heart.

Oscar and Gus charge for my Jeep, their tails wagging, barks wild with excitement. Oscar's limp from his bear-trap injury is still pronounced, but it doesn't seem to slow him down much. He reaches me as my boots hit the snow only a second later than Gus, both wolf dogs sniffing my mitten in greeting.

I give them each a head scratch. "Where's Roy, huh? In the shop?" I don't need an answer from them—not that I would get one. The curl of dark smoke from the chimney pipe is answer enough. If the sixty-something-year-old man isn't tending to the animals, he's in there, sawing and hammering and sanding wood with the deftness of a true craftsman.

The chickens cluck noisily inside their warm coop as I pass, reminding me that I need to add eggs to my grocery list. We're running low and Roy's hens aren't producing much these days, with the long nights and cold days of the Alaskan winter.

I yank open the sliding barn door, quickly closing it behind me to trap the warmth.

"You didn't tell me you were comin'!" Roy's Texan drawl is gruff as he hastily drapes a sheet over his woodworking creation, fussing with a corner to cover it completely.

"When do I ever?" Whatever he's building, he doesn't want me to see it. If I didn't know better, I'd think it might be a Christmas present. I stifle my smile and inhale the familiar smell—a blend of wood shavings and goats, infused with lingering smoke from the blazing fire in the small black stove—as I wave the envelope in my hand. "Your check came." It was waiting in our mailbox, along with a small stack of Christmas cards—mostly from customers of The Yeti—and a package from Diana.

His frown is deep, bordering on a scowl. "What check?"

"Remember? Liz sold the octopus a few weeks ago. I told you about it." The elaborate wood carving—one of countless Roy has carved over the years of living his best hermit life—was the last one on consignment at the Anchorage art shop. It fetched a mint, too. The owner is already asking me for more pieces.

His frown somehow grows deeper, his steel-gray eyes drifting over the plastic bag dangling from my fingertips. An extra loaf of banana bread I made during my baking frenzy. "Right."

"The woman who bought it is looking for a dolphin sculpture. She asked if you'd consider carving one for her. I guess she has a thing for marine animals? Anyway, she offered to pay half down in a deposit."

I expect Roy's usual refusal, his bark of "I don't do custom!" But he shakes his head and says, "I can't remember what's on the shelf. I might have one already. I'll take a look later."

It's my turn to frown. "You feeling all right?"

"Yeah. Fine. Why?"

"You seem ... distracted."

"Just busy," he mutters, rubbing his brow before looking at his soiled hands and then at the clutter of tools and dust, as if searching for something.

"Okay. Well, I'll leave the check on your counter. I'm heading into town for some last-minute groceries. You need me to pick anything up for you while I'm there?"

"No. Thank you."

Roy uses that word sparingly and always as an afterthought, as if he has to prompt himself to remember his manners. He's definitely off today.

I'm at the door when I decide to give it another shot. "You sure you don't want to come to Christmas—"

"No."

It's not the first time I've invited Roy to Christmas Day dinner over the last few weeks. The answer is always the same. I don't let that deter me. "We have plenty of room and food. And a *huge* turkey. I told Jonah twenty pounds, tops, and he went and ordered a *twenty-five* pounder. And you'd get to see us try out that table you built." A true piece of live-edge art that competes with the floor-to-ceiling stone fireplace as the focal point of our main floor.

Roy rifles through his toolbox but doesn't seem to be looking for anything in particular. "I'm good here."

"*Alone?*"

"I'm not alone. I've got the goats and the chickens, and the hounds. They're all the company I need." He pauses in his tinkering to cast a cutting look my way. "At least they won't talk my ear off."

I make sure he sees me rolling my eyes. "Suit yourself."

"Don't let the cold in behind you!"

I use all my strength to pull the barn door closed, hoping it'll shut with a bang, but the door isn't built for theatrics and it glides smoothly into place. I settle for stomping up the porch steps, pausing only long enough to fish out the miniature potted Christmas tree from my Jeep.

There was a time when Roy didn't allow anyone inside his rustic one-bedroom cabin. While he's still guarded, he no longer flinches at me coming in and out as I please, delivering food and perusing the wooden carvings that line the beautiful custom bookshelves.

I set the loaf of banana bread next to his stove and prop the check next to the can of beef stew he's set out for that night's meal. At least I know he won't miss it that way. With that done, I search for the ideal spot to set the tree. The old trunk by the window, next to the framed picture of Roy's daughter and ex-wife, seems the most ideal. I plug in the strand of white twinkle lights and then step back to admire it. I doubt this place has seen any festive joy since Roy moved here from Texas, thirty-three years ago.

Hopefully he doesn't toss it out.

A Christmas card on the kitchen table catches my eye, next to a small pile of unopened bills. My curiosity over who might send the curmudgeon holiday greetings gets the better of me. With a quick glance out the window to ensure Roy isn't on his way in, I peek inside.

My heart skips a beat at the flowery signature on the bottom.

Delyla.

His estranged daughter sent him a Christmas card? Roy told me, on one of the rare occasions he's ever mentioned his family, that they weren't on speaking terms. Was he lying? How often does Delyla send him a Christmas card? Does she do it every year?

A picture and a note lay atop the torn-open mailing envelope. I check the picture first. It's of a stunning blonde, perhaps in her thirties, dressed in black jeans and a white cable-knit sweater. Her arms are wrapped around two young children, a boy and girl, each in matching black pants and white sweaters. All three are wearing festive red cowboy hats to mark the family holiday photograph. They look the part of a perfect, happy family, though I don't miss the absence of a husband or father figure.

With another glance at the barn door, I unfold the handwritten note.

CHAPTER TWO

"She *wants* a relationship with him, Simon. Why else would she have contacted him? Why would she send pictures of his grandchildren to him?"

"I'm not suggesting she doesn't have good intentions." Simon's words, delivered in his smooth, Hugh Grant–esque British lilt, sound distant on the speakerphone as he putters around the kitchen. The clang of metal against porcelain tells me he's fixing himself a chamomile tea to help him sleep. The man is as predictable as Bandit around an unattended plate of food. "Roy may be a curiosity to her more than anything else. Or maybe there's a need for closure that's been lingering all these years. Losing a parent tends to prod us into actions we might not have planned on taking."

I sped-read through two pages of floral handwriting, afraid to get caught invading Roy's privacy. I quickly confirmed that Roy's ex-wife, Nicole, passed away from breast cancer four months ago; Delyla found her father's address while cleaning out her mother's filing cabinet and this is the first time she's ever reached out to him.

The letter seemed cordial enough—an introductory note

between two strangers, a "Dear Roy"—and yet between the lines, I sensed hours, if not days, of personal toil in choosing her words as she updated her father on the past thirty-three years of her life.

Delyla divorced three years ago after almost ten years of marriage to her high school sweetheart. Her mother, a widow after thirty happy years with a man named Jim, was complaining about being lonely, so Delyla and her children—outgoing, football-loving, seven-year-old Gavin and reserved nine-year-old artist Lauren—moved back into Delyla's childhood home. They're still there, in the same town outside Dallas where Roy and Nicole once lived together.

The kids don't see much of their father, who has already remarried, with one child and another on the way. All that in just three years? That makes me think that relationship started long before the ink dried on the divorce papers, but there's no hint of animosity hidden in Delyla's explanation to suggest an affair.

Delyla didn't ask any questions of Roy. No "Why?" or "Do you ever think about me?" No "What have you been doing for the past three decades?"

She didn't demand answers.

She didn't make accusations.

She simply ended the note with her home address, phone number, and email. An unspoken invitation for Roy to reach out, should he so choose, I gather. But she never came right out and asked him to.

Roy was rattled this afternoon. I can't tell if it's Nicole's death or receiving a letter from his long-lost daughter that caused that. Likely both.

"I wouldn't get too hopeful about this if I were you, Calla, especially given the kind of man Roy is. There's a lot of bad history to unpack. Who knows what she's grown up hearing about her father?"

"I'm not. I don't even know what Roy's going to do with this information. Probably nothing." While he's far less prickly than he used to be, he still goes out of his way to keep people out of reach.

Beams of headlights flash across a window, signaling Jonah's return from Anchorage. A nervous flutter stirs in my stomach. "They're here!" It comes out in a squeal.

Simon's soft chuckle soothes me. "Don't worry. They're going to love you. And if they don't? We'll be there the day after tomorrow to talk some sense into them."

I smile. "Pack enough warm clothes! This big storm rolling in over Christmas is supposed to be bad." I never paid much attention to the weather. Living in Alaska? I don't roll out of bed without checking the weather online.

"Bigger than last year?"

I recall the nightmare of being stranded in Anchorage, ready to spend my Christmas holiday with strangers and a vast collection of stuffed wildlife. "As long as it comes after you arrive, I don't care if we get ten feet."

"Well, you know your mother. Clothing has never been an issue for us. She made me haul out a third suitcase. Of course, some of that space is reserved for her bridal magazine collection."

I groan. While I'm anxious to see my mom again, I'm dreading the pressure to set a wedding date. For a woman who spent so much effort warning me against the perils of falling in love with a bush pilot who lives across the continent, she has certainly changed her tune.

"I know. Just try to remember that you're her *only* daughter. All she wants is for you to have the day of your dreams, and for her to be able to help you plan it."

"Yeah. In *Toronto*." She's been relentless, sending website links of possible reception venues and photographers almost daily.

"She has a lot of connections here, being in the floristry. Connections she doesn't have in Alaska."

"But having it in Alaska might make more sense for *us*."

"Then that is what you tell her, and she'll accept it." He adds after a beat, "Eventually."

I hear Jonah's booming voice. "I should go. Love you." I end the call with Simon and rush to jam another log in the dwindling fire.

"... small fortune to heat, but we're actually using it a lot more in the winter than I thought we would."

They must be talking about the hot tub—a focal point on the cozy screened-in porch and a place Jonah and I have grown accustomed to enjoying sans bathing suits, something we won't be doing for the next two weeks.

Dusting my hands off on my jeans, I venture to the entrance, tamping down the nerves that come with meeting your future mother-in-law in person for the first time.

Jonah's looming presence fills the foyer, chilled air curling around him. "Hey, babe." He leans in to kiss me chastely, his icy-blue eyes twinkling with something—excitement? nervousness? —before shifting out of the way to reveal two people who look like they've traveled thousands of miles and eleven time zones to get here. His throat bobs with a hard swallow. "Mom, this is—"

"Calla." My name is a heavy sigh on Astrid's voice. Her shoulders sag, as if she's been waiting for this moment forever and is relieved it's finally here. She reaches out with cool hands to grasp mine, squeezing them tightly for a brief moment. "It's *so good* to meet you."

"It is," I agree with a widening smile, the lilt in her accent a familiar sound after a dozen phone calls in preparation for this visit.

I've only seen a few pictures of Astrid, one being the framed photograph from Jonah's house in Bangor that now resides on a bookshelf in the corner. In that one, taken when Jonah was a scrawny little boy in Anchorage, Astrid resembled a fashion model—tall and thin, with long, white-blonde hair. Another picture from Jonah's high school graduation showed her as a slightly older version of the Norwegian stunner in the cherry-red bikini.

Now, at fifty-nine, the years are claiming their marks on this regal-looking woman. She still holds herself with statuesque grace, but with a healthy layer of meat and muscle on her bones. Crow's-feet and frown lines that my mother aggressively keeps at bay with regular Botox injections crinkle Astrid's skin with ease. I doubt a needle has ever touched that glowing skin. And her once-long hair has been cropped short but stylish, the platinum color surely the product of a salon.

"This is Björn." She gestures at the white-haired man of the same height beside her. Standing side by side, the decade in age difference between them is glaring.

"I'm sure you've heard *many* wonderful things about me." Björn's cerulean eyes cut to his stepson, and even with the accent, there's no mistaking the dig. But when his gaze shifts back to me, I see nothing but polite weariness. "It's so nice to meet the woman who managed to tame Astrid's son." He offers me his hand and I take it, earning myself a firm handshake.

"I don't know how well he's been tamed, but ..." I force my smile wider. "It's so nice to meet you both. Come in and get warm. I have a lasagna in the oven." I nod toward the table, set for four, a bottle of red already cracked and breathing.

"We've already eaten." Björn's head is shaking. "I just want my bed."

Astrid shoots him with a brief but sharp look, with blue eyes that match Jonah's. "Thank you, Calla. We ate in Seattle while we were waiting for the next plane. We wanted to stop in and say hello, but we're both quite tired. Especially this old man."

"Of course. No worries."

"I'm gonna take them over to the cabin." Jonah reaches for the keys to the old beat-up pickup—I still think of it as Phil's. "You mind giving me a ride back?"

"At your service." I collect the keys from his hand and a kiss from his lips, and trail Astrid and Björn out the door.

"They were supposed to be here this week to route the internet so you'd have Wi-Fi, but they rescheduled until early January. Texts still come, sporadically. They're just … spotty." At best. During bad weather, it's basically a dead zone.

"We'll survive." Astrid inhales deeply, her eyes searching the cabin's wooden interior with interest. "Smells like freshly cut wood."

I laugh, my own gaze taking in the small space, finished with compact Scandinavian-style furnishings and a blend of punchy Navajo blankets and rugs to add color. I even tucked a small Christmas tree into the corner and strung tiny white lights around the windows to help with the holiday atmosphere. "Yeah, it's about as fresh as it can get. Roy finished the trim last weekend."

"And we were still moving shit in here up until yesterday. Calla worked her butt off to get it ready in time. You should have everything you need." Jonah stomps the snow off his boots and then lugs two large suitcases, one in each hand. He hauls each onto the stands I ordered—that took two months to arrive—grunting under the weight. "Jesus, what'd you bring with you?"

"It's Christmas. I wasn't going to arrive empty-handed," Astrid says matter-of-factly.

"You remember that we have stores here, right?"

She reaches up to rest her palm against her son's cheek. "But not Norwegian stores, *vennen*."

I don't know what she called him, but it seems to strike a chord because Jonah's stern expression softens. He ropes his arms around his mother's shoulders, pulling her into his chest.

She responds instantly, curling her arms around his waist. "I forgot how big you are. Karl and Ivar are tiny by comparison."

Those names I recognize as Björn's sons, whom Jonah cares for about as much as he does Björn, though I've never received a solid reason why his annoyance extends that far. Sometimes I wonder if his dislike for his stepbrothers is rooted in jealousy. Jonah grew up an only child; he's not used to sharing his mom. Worse, Karl and Ivar and their families live within a ten-minute drive of Astrid and Björn. They eat dinner together once a week and spend their holidays together.

"I missed you," he murmurs.

"That's because you haven't seen me in—how long has it been again? *Three* years?"

He grins sheepishly. "Four."

"Ah. *Four* years since you've seen your own mother. I'm surprised you even found me at the airport." Her tone is soft, playful, her eyes twinkling as she chides her only son.

Yet, I can't help but wonder if her words are laced with a hint of bitterness. Astrid may have two stepsons and five step-grandchildren to keep her occupied, but Jonah is her only biological child. Since leaving Las Vegas for Alaska when he was twenty-one, he has only seen his mother three times—once, to witness her marry a man he doesn't care for. Three times in eleven years, and apparently the two trips to Oslo were riddled with bickering and shouting matches. The last time, he finished off his stay in a hotel.

The four-year gap since his last visit isn't entirely his fault, though. Jonah was supposed to fly to Norway for Christmas last year, but he canceled after learning of my father's terminal illness. Then again, my dad passed in September. Plenty of time to rebook, but Jonah chose to stay close for Agnes and Mabel's sake, even before he made the surprise trip to Toronto to lure me back to the wild.

Still, *four years* since he's held his mother.

Does she resent him for that? She did move all the way to Oslo. But before that, Jonah moved to Alaska.

It's been *one* year since I last saw my mother, and almost every time we speak she likes to remind me that I chose to move thousands of miles away.

"I brought a bunch of wood in for the fire and there's more on the side, but the Toyostove will keep you guys warm through the night," Jonah explains, heading for the woodstove. He lit it before he left for the airport, but only hot embers glow now, the log long since burned.

"It's toasty in here." Astrid rubs her hands together, contradicting her words. "I forgot how cold it gets in Alaska. It was raining when we left Oslo."

"It's been colder than usual." And the news is forecasting a bitter front trailing in behind the coming storm. "I've stocked the fridge with everything I thought you might need, but if there's anything else, just let us know. There are plenty of blankets and towels and pillows. Everything."

"I'm sure we'll be fine, Calla. Don't worry yourself."

"And let me know what you think about the bed." I plan on listing the cabin on the rental site in January for weekend renters looking for a winter escape. Astrid and Björn are our guinea pigs.

"For what she paid, that mattress better come with servants that tuck you in at night and sing you lullabies," Jonah grumbles, earning my exasperated eye roll.

Astrid chuckles. "I don't think we'll need any lullabies tonight. I'm half-asleep already."

The toilet flushes and after a brief rush of the tap water, Björn emerges from the bathroom. "It feels like a coffin in there. How long have we been banished out here? The whole two weeks?"

Astrid rhymes off something in Norwegian that sounds musical but coupled with her sharp glare is clearly an admonishment. She switches back to English to say, "It's *fine*. It's perfect for us. Ignore him. He's old and grumpy and doesn't like to leave home."

Jonah stoops to tuck a log into the woodstove, muttering, "He should have stayed there, then."

"So, not only do you make your mother fly halfway across the world if she wants to see you, but now you want her to do it *alone*?" Björn snipes back.

"If you're going to complain for the next two weeks, then yeah. And she's *more than capable* of traveling on her own. She doesn't *need* you."

Björn stabs the air with his index finger. "If you knew what—"

"Enough!" Astrid's hands raise in the air, her brow pinched with strain. "Don't start already. *Please*. It's been a *very* long day."

I loop my arms around Jonah's biceps and gently guide him toward the door. "We'll let you get settled." Though, from the sounds of it, I'm not sure Björn will be comfortable here. That's a bit of a pinprick to my bubble of enthusiasm over this cabin's completion.

Astrid dips her head to me. "Calla, thank you so much for making all these efforts for our comfort. Everything is *perfect*. We'll see you in the morning."

"Come over whenever you're up. The door'll be unlocked." Jonah dangles the key to the pickup truck before hanging it on the wall hook. "It's all gassed up. I'll plug in the block heater on our way out. Don't forget to unplug it."

Astrid smiles. "Oh, I forgot about those days."

I remember as we reach the door. "Oh! If you happen to see two big dogs that look like wolves running around, don't panic. They're harmless."

Björn's bushy gray eyebrows arch. "Are they wolves or are they dogs?"

"A bit of both, probably, but the official answer is malamute." That's Roy's *bullshit* answer, to keep the gossip at bay and officers off his back.

Björn nods slowly. "I've always liked malamutes."

"There's actually something he *does* like," Jonah mutters under his breath.

I herd him out with a hand on his back before he can spark another argument.

CHAPTER THREE

"It *is* really small, but I didn't have a lot to work with. Do you think renters will mind?"

"People aren't gonna rent that place so they can hang out in the bathroom." Jonah's words are garbled thanks to the toothbrush in his mouth.

"You're right." I study the draft listing on the Airbnb site. I've been working on it for weeks. "Still ... maybe I should mention it?" But what would I say? *Warning: Coffin-sized bathroom?* I sigh. "Do you really think they'll be comfortable over there? Because they can stay here. I know your mom insisted, but it doesn't sound as if Björn—"

"Fuck Björn!" The tap shuts off with a dull thud. A moment later, Jonah emerges, scowling. "It's *perfect,* Calla. It's got a toilet, a sink, and a shower. What the hell else does he need? *Nothing.* He just wants to find things to bitch about. That's what he does. Complains about *everything.* I warned you he would, didn't I?"

"You did."

The mattress sinks beneath Jonah's weight as he slides into his side of our bed. "Don't let him get inside your head. You've worked your ass off to get that place ready in time for them.

Look at this." He scrolls through the pictures I took of the cabin yesterday with Simon's trusty Canon. "It's gonna be the nicest rental within a hundred miles of Trapper's Crossing."

"It *is* nice."

Jonah sinks back into his pillow. "The least the dickhead could do is be respectful."

I roll my eyes. "Okay, you need to ease up, Jonah, or these two weeks are going to feel twice as long and *nobody* will enjoy themselves. Especially not your mother."

"Yeah, I know. He just pushes my buttons so easily."

"Still. You need to bite your tongue."

"When have I *ever* been able to do that?"

"Never." I love that about Jonah. *Usually.*

He smiles, but it falls off quickly. "He refused to let me pick them up in the plane, but then he complained the entire way here."

"About what?"

"About *everything.* The two-hour drive, the music on the radio, the Jeep being too bumpy and cramped and not good in the snow. Which I agree with—"

I groan. "Don't start this again."

"I'm worried about you going off the road."

I shake my head. One snowfall in October and Jonah decided he didn't like the way my Jeep Wrangler—a birthday gift from him—handles the slippery terrain. "There's *nothing wrong* with my Jeep. It's literally designed for handling bad roads."

"Fine. I'm worried about *you* handling the bad roads, okay?"

My mouth drops open. The truth comes out. "I'm a *good* driver!"

"You drive too fast."

"I do not! And that is *so rich,* coming from you."

"Oh yeah?" He smirks. "How many winters have you driven in?"

"That's not the point." Neither is the fact that I backed into a moose on my driving test, and if he brings that up right now, I will scream.

"If I were flying a plane recklessly, you wouldn't want me up there anymore."

"Uh, you *crashed two* planes," I remind him dryly. "Have I told you to stop flying?"

"That wasn't my—"

"Ah!" I raise a pointed finger at him.

His lips twist as he searches for a suitable retort that he can't make because one of those crashes *was* his fault. He wasn't being smart.

I school my tone, because we're about to end up in a shouting match. "It's *my* Jeep. I *love* my Jeep. I'm *not* selling it, and I'm not driving ten miles an hour. If *you* don't want to drive it, buy yourself a nice, new, reliable truck. We have the money."

I get a flat look in return, but it doesn't seem Jonah's in the mood to argue. "Anyway, I told Björn he could have rented a car and driven himself instead of getting door-to-door valet service."

"What'd he say to that?"

"That he already spent enough money on plane tickets, and he shouldn't have to rent a car, too."

"Flying from Oslo to Alaska isn't cheap." I know because I looked up the cost. I was going to offer to pay for their flights. Jonah talked me out of it, saying Björn would consider it an insult.

He waves my words away. "The stingy bastard has plenty of money. He just wants to complain because he's a miserable prick."

"He didn't seem *that bad*." Grouchy, sure. A bit abrupt, maybe. "Plus, he's sixty-nine and he's probably been awake for a day and a half. I'd be miserable, too."

Jonah frowns at me. "When did you become so tolerant?"

I laugh. "Shut up."

"I'm serious. You've been hangin' around Muriel and Roy too much. They've conditioned you to put up with too much shit."

"Oh! Speaking of Roy ... I haven't had a chance to tell you yet." I shut my laptop and set it on the nightstand, then slither in next to Jonah. He lifts his arm without prompting, allowing me a spot to rest my head against his broad chest.

I relay the details of Delyla's letter.

"So, you're telling me you snooped through a highly private man's personal mail?"

"It was right *there*."

"That's something Muriel would do."

"It's not the same!"

"Okay, Mini Muriel."

I swat his stomach playfully and his muscles tense. "She would have stormed back out to the barn and badgered him with questions. *I* didn't do that."

"Because he'd probably threaten you with his gun."

"Whatever. Anyway, none of this is the point."

Jonah smiles, as if humoring me. "Okay. What's the point?"

"He's not going to contact her."

"And that's his choice. It's his business. We don't know what happened between him and his family all those years ago. Maybe he doesn't want anything to do with them."

I bite my tongue against the urge to say that, actually, we do know. *I* know, because Roy told me, that dreaded night back in August when Jonah's plane crashed in the valley. I've never repeated what Roy shared to anyone but Simon, and I did that because Simon doesn't judge.

Jonah would judge. Harshly.

Roy has already done an adequate job of punishing himself, isolated in his cabin in the woods for the past thirty-three years, relying on barn animals and feral dogs for companionship.

"What about forgiving past crimes and letting go? Aren't you the one who pushed me to give my father another chance?" And

Jonah did that because he didn't give his father another chance until it was too late.

"Yeah, but Roy's not dying. Besides, Wren was a decent guy. Roy is … Roy."

"Roy's decent."

Jonah snorts. "Last week, when he came by to trim Zeke's hooves, he was wearing that goddamn raccoon-fur hat again. Bandit wouldn't come out."

"He's decent in his own way," I amend. "And, you know, I was thinking, if Agnes hadn't taken it upon herself to call me, *I* never would have come to Alaska. I never would have gotten to know my dad before he died. *We* never would have met."

"So?" Jonah's voice has taken on a wary edge.

"So … I took a picture of Delyla's contact info."

He rolls, shifting me onto my back. "What kind of crazy plan is going on in that pretty head of yours?"

"I don't know yet."

His fingers stroke my hair off my face before he peers down at me. "He's not like Wren was, though. He's more like a wild animal. One that *finally* trusts you. That can all be erased in a blink if you do something to break his trust, and you'll be back to square one with him."

"I know. That's what I'm worried about." Roy has come so far since that first visit back in March, the day we moved in and found out we were proud owners of a goat we didn't want.

"Enough about Roy." Jonah leans in, his lips grazing my jawline, shifting to the sensitive spot below my ear. He knows that's a weak spot of mine. "It's our second-to-last night alone until January *second*."

"Oh my God, you're right!"

"That's a *long* time to have your mother and Simon on the other side of our bedroom wall."

"They both wear earplugs to sleep." Simon is a light sleeper, and the sound of him breathing irritates my mother.

"Earplugs won't drown you out."

"Oh, shut up." Jonah loves to tease me about how loud I can get, but it's—usually—not true. "I guess you better get to work, then."

He gives me a questioning look. "Get to work with what, exactly?"

"You owe me." I waggle my eyebrows. "For yesterday, in the office."

The corner of his mouth kicks up as his fingers deftly unfasten the buttons of my pajama top, until he's casting the sides open, uncovering my breasts to the cool air. "Have I ever told you how much I love all these sexy, oversized flannel pajamas you keep buying for yourself? Especially the ones with the candy canes?"

My laughter carries from deep in my belly as he shifts his broad body down, his tongue leaving a wet trail along my skin, from my collarbone all the way to my belly button, pausing for a few swirls around my peaked nipples. "Good, because I bought two more pairs." I pause, and then add in a playfully seductive voice, "Vennen."

He freezes. "Can you not call me that? Especially not when I'm doing *this*?"

"Okay, vennen," I echo, stifling my giggle.

"Seriously."

"What does it mean?"

"It's a term of endearment. For a little *boy*." He tugs my bottoms off in one fell swoop of his hand and then tosses them away. Shifting over to fit his shoulders between my thighs, he pauses to stare steadily into my eyes. "Do I look like a little boy to you, Calla?" His voice has grown husky.

I swallow my amusement away. "No." He looks like the most masculine, beautiful man I've ever laid eyes on.

I inhale sharply at the first swipe of his tongue.

"What the *hell* are you talking about? Mom? What is he talking about!"

I blink the sleep from my eyes and check the clock to see that it's only eight A.M. It's still dark out, but Björn and Astrid have probably been up for hours, given the time difference.

With a groan, I slide out of bed, shuddering against the morning chill. I hastily clean myself up in the bathroom and then rush downstairs.

"Why am I finding out now? From *him*?" Jonah is glaring at Björn from across the kitchen island, but he's clearly talking to his mother, perched on a kitchen stool.

"I didn't want to worry you for something so minor," Astrid responds calmly, flipping through an urban bridal magazine Diana subscribed me to as soon as Jonah and I got engaged. Her face is freshly made with mascara and a hint of lipstick, her short, platinum-blonde hair styled for the day, yet the expression she wears is heavy with exhaustion. Whether it's from her long travels or this ongoing strife between her son and husband, only she can tell.

Meanwhile, Jonah looks like he's been slapped across the face as he shakes his head at his mother. "Minor? You call that *minor*?"

Astrid's gaze stalls on an image of wedding dresses as she says something to Björn in Norwegian. Again, that musical lilt masks what I'm assuming are unpleasant words.

"Because I'm not keeping your secrets anymore!" he snaps in English, likely for Jonah's benefit.

"Watch your tone with her!" Jonah snaps back.

My body stiffens with the rising voices. If this continues, there will be nuclear war–level tension by Christmas Day.

I take the last two steps and holler, "Good morning," hoping my presence might defuse the impending explosion. "How did everyone sleep?"

Astrid answers with a warm, albeit embarrassed smile. "Not bad. We're still on Oslo time. It'll probably take us a full week to adapt." She adds a moment later, "But the cabin is quite comfortable. Right, Björn?" Her eyebrows arch as she looks to her husband.

"Yes. Comfortable." Whether he's been schooled on the appropriate answer or not, I appreciate it.

"Morning." I stretch on my tiptoes to reach Jonah's lips for a morning kiss before flashing a three-second warning look at him. When I see the glimmer of recognition there—that he needs to calm down—I continue to the barista machine for a much-needed caffeine jolt.

"I have a run up near Talkeetna this morning that I need to get ready for, but then I can help you guys move your things over here," Jonah offers, his tone adjusted accordingly. "You can have the room we set up for Agnes and Mabel."

I frown at his back. What is going on? Didn't Astrid just say they were comfortable in the cabin?

"There's no need—"

"I'll be back around one." Jonah rounds the counter and leans in to kiss his mother on the forehead. "Have everything packed if you can, okay?"

She sighs but then reaches up to graze her son's cheek. "Okay, vennen."

Despite the curious change of plans, I stifle the urge to giggle.

Without so much as a glance at Björn, Jonah marches out the side door, stalling only long enough to grab his winter hat and gloves from the hook. Seconds later, the snowmachine's engine purrs, cutting into the awkward silence in the kitchen.

What secret did Björn divulge? What has Astrid been keeping from her son?

"That is quite the contraption," Astrid murmurs through a sip of her coffee, her attention on the barista machine. "I think I will need to read the manual to figure it out."

"Would you like me to make you something? Latte, cappuccino, espresso ..."

She waves the offer away. "We're fine with our black coffee."

"Are you hungry? I have homemade banana loaf." I pull it out of the fridge and set it on the counter, along with plates. I spent the last week stocking the house with enough food to feed twenty people with twenty different eating habits. "Or I could make you some eggs and bacon. Or, we have fruit salad and yogurt, if you'd rather—"

"This is fine." She reaches for the knife to cut Björn a slice of bread. She slides the plate to him without a word and he settles down on the stool without so much as a thank-you. "Jonah said you have a Christmas party to attend tonight?"

"Yeah. I got roped into helping with the big annual charity dinner at the community center. I'm sorry, I couldn't get out of it—"

"Why would you need to get out of it?" She cuts me off abruptly with a frown. "It sounds like an important night."

"Well, it is, but you guys just got here and I feel bad about leaving you all alone."

"If you keep fussing over us, you'll be exhausted and counting down the days until we leave." She softens her admonishment with a smile. "So, what do you have to do for this dinner?"

"I don't know, actually. Probably a lot of grunt work. Muriel told me to be there at ten."

"Is that the bossy neighbor?"

"Yeah. She's in charge of planning the night. She asked for my help." More like told me I was helping, after recognizing that my marketing plans *might* have had a hand in the smashing success of the Winter Carnival—with record attendance and its highest earnings in fifty years. "Teddy dresses up as Santa."

She quietly admonishes Björn as she picks at wayward banana-bread crumbs on the counter around his plate. "Is that the grouchy neighbor?"

"No. That's Roy." I laugh at the thought of Roy donning a red suit and white beard. He'd be Billy Bob Thornton's version of Santa. He'd be a child's worst nightmare. "Teddy is Muriel's husband, and he's probably the happiest man I've ever met—oh, crap! He forgot his thermos." I spy the tall navy-blue cylinder sitting by the coffee pot. Jonah has taken to filling it on his way out the door in the morning, without fail. Whatever they were fighting over before I came down distracted him.

"Go, go ..." Astrid ushers me away. "Bring it to him, before he flies off. We can talk more when you come back. Maybe about setting a wedding date?" She reaches for the magazine. "So perhaps those who are traveling twenty hours to see their *only* son get married have sufficient time to prepare?" It sounds like a suggestion, but the cutting glance she follows it up with tells me she doesn't plan on boarding that plane home without arrangements etched into her calendar.

Björn mutters something in Norwegian to Astrid. It doesn't sound nearly as musical in his gruff voice.

She collects his plate and puts it in the sink.

And I fill Jonah's thermos with black coffee, thankful for an excuse to track him down and find out what's going on.

CHAPTER FOUR

Toby's burgundy pickup truck is parked outside the hangar when I sail in on the green snowmachine that has unofficially become mine. Now that the regular fishing season is closed and Trapper's Crossing Resort is without guests, he's been able to dedicate more time to working on Phil's old plane, coming here early in the day, before the mechanics shop where he services small engines gets busy.

Toby and Jonah are standing beside the 1959 Beaver when I stroll through the side door. They turn in unison at the intrusion.

"You forgot this." I wave the thermos in the air.

"Yeah. I realized halfway here, but there was no way I was goin' back to deal with them again."

By "them," I know he means Björn. Still, I shoot him a disapproving look before turning my attention to the burly thirty-five-year-old. Toby was my first friend when we moved to Trapper's Crossing this past March, back when I was still struggling with acclimating to this isolated place. "Didn't think I'd see you here today, with the Christmas dinner happening later."

"Yeah." He scratches the brown scruff on his chin. Come May, he'll be clean-shaven again, but until then, he'll let it grow all winter. "I just stopped by to double-check on a part I've been trying to find."

"How long is the task list Muriel has for you?"

His face splits into that wide grin that instantly softens his features. "Two pages, front and back."

And yet I'm sure he didn't utter a word of complaint, even when his mother would deserve it. The man is as kindhearted as his father and always willing to offer a hand. I laugh. "Good luck."

His grin grows wider. "She's got one for you, too, and it's longer."

"Don't tell me that," I groan.

"Sorry. Figured you should be prepared."

"So, you're thinking you'll have it by Monday?" Jonah asks, steering the conversation back to plane talk.

"They said they'd try to get it here before the storm. Once I get it, I can start putting this baby back together." He gives the loose engine a pat.

"When do you think we'll have it in the air again?"

Toby shrugs. "Hard to say. Last I heard, seats will be back by late January, but that's more an estimate. I should have everything else ready by then, barring any more surprises."

"Perfect." Jonah's blue gaze drags over the carcass of the plane. It's in pieces and looking like it belongs in a scrapyard. "And then all it needs is a fresh coat of paint."

"You want to paint it?" Toby studies the plane's body, which I'll admit is already in decent condition.

"Canary yellow," Jonah answers without a moment's hesitation. "That was Wren's favorite color, and that's this guy's name."

And if Jonah is anything, it's sentimental. Surprisingly so.

I close the distance to rope my arms around his waist. "He would love it."

He returns the affection, pulling me tight against his chest.

Toby's phone chirps in his pocket. He checks the message and, by the soft grunt that escapes, I can tell it's Muriel, beckoning. "Well, I better head out now. See you in a few, Calla?"

"With bells on. *Literally*." Volunteers are required to wear elf costumes. I haven't seen mine but Emily warned me to be ready for a lot of jingling.

Toby's chuckle follows him out the door.

"Thanks for this." Jonah slips the thermos from my hand and kisses me in one smooth motion before peeling away. "I should get going."

I hook my hand around his arm, stalling his escape. "Not before you tell me what that was back there. Why are they staying in Agnes and Mabel's room, if the cabin is okay?"

Jonah pauses to pinch the bridge of his nose as if in pain. "My mom had a pulmonary embolism last year, in August."

"Oh, wow. That's … bad, right?" I stumble over my words. I don't actually know what that is, but I'm doing the math—last August was just before my father died. "That's something to do with her lungs?"

"A blockage, yeah. She started having chest pain, so they rushed her to the hospital and ran all the tests. They found a blood clot. A pretty big one."

"Did she have to have surgery?"

He shakes his head. "I don't know. Something to do with a catheter put into her lung to feed medicine in to break up the clot. It sounds like surgery to me, but she said she was awake through it. Then they put her on blood thinners. Her blood clots really fast. It's always been like that. She'll probably have to take the thinners for the rest of her life."

"Is she doing okay *now*?"

"She says she is, but who the fuck really knows. She didn't tell me about this, so what else isn't she telling me about?" Jonah is scowling. "Björn should have called me."

"It sounds like she told him not to."

"I don't care. He should have told me, anyway." He paces

around the plane engine. "I'm her *son*."

"You're right. Someone should have told you. But why do you think she might not have? What would you have done?"

"I would have gone to Oslo!"

"Right."

He seems to consider that for a long moment. "I would have flown back the second she told me, and then I might have not been there for Wren when he died. Or you."

I'm not sure what to say to ease Jonah's frustration. If that had been my mother or Simon, I would be just as furious to find out more than a year after the fact.

"And then fucking Björn"—he spits his name out like a curse—"he has the nerve to lay a guilt trip on me for making her fly all the way here to see me when I had no clue this was going on in the first place! Like, of course I would never have agreed to this, had I known! She shouldn't be flying halfway across the world! Long plane rides are a risk for people with her condition. What if the thinners stop working and she's out there, in the middle of the night, with a huge blood clot working through her veins? And she can't even get a signal to call for help."

"That's why you want them staying at our house." The pieces are beginning to fit together.

"At least if she's in our house and something goes wrong, I'm there."

Whether that's a legitimate concern, I'm not sure. What I do know is that Jonah won't sleep a wink with her across the lake.

"It's the right decision. I'll call Agnes and give her the heads-up. She won't mind. Mabel was whining that she wanted to stay out there, anyway." Though that was before she learned that the Wi-Fi setup was delayed.

"Thanks." He nods slowly. "It caught me off guard. I didn't think I'd have to start worrying about her health yet. She's still so young."

"And it sounds like she has things under control." I reach up to comb his freshly groomed beard with my fingertips. "She'll be fine."

"Yeah?" He sounds doubtful.

"Yeah. Susan, Simon, Astrid, and Björn under one roof. What could go wrong?"

He tips his head back with a groan. "Besides Björn calling Simon a quack?"

"Besides that." Björn doesn't hide the fact that he thinks psychiatrists are fake doctors.

"Maybe Björn can stay in the cabin by himself."

"Stop it." I laugh as I stretch on tiptoes to kiss his lips.

I ease my Jeep into the row of parked vehicles at the Trapper's Crossing community center at twenty-five past ten, preparing myself for grief about my tardiness. Muriel doesn't differentiate between paid positions and a person graciously volunteering their entire Saturday before Christmas. In her eyes, a job's a job and you give it your all, no matter what.

At least the sun is shining.

Collecting my things—and my energy, because something tells me I'm going to be exhausted by the time I see the inside of this Jeep again—I hop out into the frigid day. A bang pulls my attention to the left, to the outdoor rink where a group of kids whip around the ice, hockey sticks in hand, practicing their shots on net.

Marie strolls out the doors of the community center. Bonnie Hatchett is on her heels.

My stomach twinges the way it always does when I first see the beautiful blonde veterinarian, though the reaction isn't nearly as visceral as it used to be.

"What do you mean? You *saw* him do this?" Marie asks.

"Well … *no*." Bonnie presses her thin lips together in a frown.

"But we *all* know those dogs aren't bein' treated well. Who does he think he is, anyway? Showing up here, buying up all that land with no regard for anyone else." Her tone bleeds with bitterness.

"Just because you see him as direct competition to Harry's business doesn't mean you can throw around accusations of animal abuse," Marie says gently. "Not unless you have proof."

"And what if we find proof? You'll help us then, right?" Bonnie pushes.

Marie's sigh reveals her forced patience. "If you have proof, I'll see what I can do. Look, I've got to go. I have appointments all afternoon."

Bonnie doesn't seem to hear the reluctance in Marie's voice because she nods vigorously and offers, "Thank you, Dr. Lehr. Thank you for your help."

Marie notices me approaching then and picks up speed to reach me.

"What was *that* about?" I ask curiously.

Marie barely stifles her groan. "Some young hotshot moved here a few months ago and bought up the Danson property, down the road from the Hatchetts'. Apparently, he's breeding sled dogs." She turns to watch the tiny, hunched woman climb into an old Dodge pickup. "Bonnie claims he's abusing them."

"Do you believe her?"

Marie shrugs. "Who knows? It happens. But Bonnie's son also breeds sled dogs, and something tells me business hasn't been good for him lately, so competition down the road is the last thing they need. Plus, this new guy won some big sled dog race wherever he's from, and he's signed up for the Iditarod."

"Didn't her son win that this year?" It seems like everyone around here has a family member racing in the annual world-famous event.

"He came in second. But he's a favorite for the coming year." Marie gives me a look. "*Was* a favorite. Now the new guy might throw a wrench into that."

I whistle. "The high-stakes drama of Alaska's sled dog world."

"Right?" Marie laughs as she slips off a mitten to push strands of her long, silky blonde hair off her face. "And the Hatchetts are trying to drag *me* into the middle of this because they know I could never ignore hearing about an abused animal." Even now, her jaw is taut with tension at the suggestion.

"So, are you going to go over to this guy's house to check it out?"

She throws her arms in the air in resignation. "Yeah. Probably, knowing me."

I smile. My father once called Marie a crusader, flying from village to village, treating animals that otherwise wouldn't receive care. At the time, she was just a friend of Jonah's, and Jonah was still just the bullheaded yeti, determined to put me back on a plane for Toronto. But the moment I met the beautiful blonde veterinarian, I knew immediately that friends or not, she was in love with him. The problem was, by that point, I was falling hard for him, too.

Since then, Marie and I have had our jealous ups and downs, all rooted in love for one man. While we'll never be *best* friends, we've become so adept at this friendly dance around each other that even I'm beginning to think it could be genuine.

I eye the double doors of Trapper's Crossing community center, banked by urns dressed in bouquets of evergreen branches and donated white twinkle lights. Free décor is the best décor, Muriel proclaimed gleefully, ever the thrifty one. "Did you see Muriel when you went in there?"

"You mean Sergeant?" Marie continues on to her truck. "She's been here since before six. When I left, she was badgering Toby to ask Emily out to dinner."

I groan. "You think that's a line item on her clipboard?"

"As long as my name's not a part of that task, she can set him up with whoever *she* deems acceptable."

I shake my head. While Marie hasn't come out and said it, I

think the idea of Muriel as a mother-in-law played a part in why she and Toby never made it past two dates. Lord knows it would scare any sane person away. Poor Toby might be a bachelor for life if he sticks around here.

Marie's truck engine starts with a roar. "Say hi to Jonah for me," she hollers before slamming her door shut.

I'm huddled in my jacket as I head for the double doors, shivering against the cold.

Muriel once called the community center the hub of the town, and there isn't a better way to describe it. Between the farmers' market and planning the Winter Carnival, I've spent so much time within these old walls, the flickering fluorescent lights and musty smell have become familiar, and almost comforting.

I enter the large hall to "Silent Night" playing over the speaker system and a flurry of activity buzzing throughout. Toby and a local named Benjamin are unfolding the last of the round dinner tables, while Emily and two other volunteers arrange chairs, ten to a table. On the far end of the room, next to the seventeen-foot Christmas tree that's been up for the whole of the Winter Carnival, Teddy and the photographer are setting up the props around Santa's ornate chair. All along the perimeter of the large room, long, rectangular tables that will be used to display items for a silent auction are already half full of donations, everything from gift baskets to handmade socks to painted mountain landscapes.

And at the center of it all is my stocky neighbor, in her usual rolled-up jeans—on account of her short legs—and a flannel button-down shirt that barely closes over her ample chest. I can always tell when she's just washed her hair because her gray curls are tight against her scalp.

"Hey, Muriel," I call out.

She spins on her heels at the sound of my voice and makes an overt display of checking her watch. "Glad to see you could join us today, Calla."

I've long since learned not to let Muriel's abrasive personality get under my skin. Her words carry no malice. It's who she is. "Sorry. Jonah's mom wants to do some baking today, so I had to dig through my cupboards. I didn't want her running out to the store if she didn't need to."

"Oh." Muriel nods, as if she approves of my excuse for the tardiness. "And how is everyone getting on over there so far?"

"Fine." Aside from Jonah wanting to strangle his stepfather, but I'm not getting into family drama with Muriel. "They're still getting settled."

"I remember holidays with my in-laws. It was a stressful time every year." She shakes her head. "Teddy's mother was something else. You've never met a more controlling woman in your life, I'll tell ya. He's lucky I have as much patience as I do, or we might never have gotten married."

A bark of laughter sounds nearby. Toby, within earshot of our conversation.

"What's so funny over there?" Muriel's eyes narrow at her son. "You got somethin' to say?"

I'm struggling to not let my own amusement slip. "So, Muriel, where do you want me to start?"

She turns back to her clipboard, dragging a stubby finger down the left margin. "You can start on the table settings."

"Perfect." Something I actually enjoy.

"The linens are in the storage room in the back. Centerpieces are in the big green containers in the corner. There's no need to get fancy with them," she warns. "We have three candles per table and enough—No! Not *that* background!" she hollers at Teddy.

He pauses to frown at the snowy landscape scene behind Santa's chair, scratching his natural long, white beard. "What's wrong with this one?"

"We did that one last year."

"Well, *I* didn't know that."

"You were *here*!" Muriel huffs and storms off toward him,

clipboard tucked under her arm. "We alternate. This year is the fireplace background."

As much as I pity Teddy, at least Muriel is too distracted with him to hound after me.

"They have this same argument every year." Toby adjusts the table nearest me a few inches to the left, an amused smirk on his face. "Every year, he puts up the wrong one."

I frown. "*Every* year?"

"Every year," Emily chirps, smiling at Toby on her way past.

Toby chuckles. "So, how are things *really* going over at your place?" He sees my expression and nods. "Yeah, Jonah seemed off this morning."

"He got some news he wasn't happy about." I tell Toby about Astrid's health surprise and Jonah's mounting guilt over her flying here.

"Shit."

"She says it's not a big deal, but …" I shrug.

"It's his mom," Toby finishes off.

"Exactly." And as wild as Jonah can be sometimes when it comes to his own safety, he is overprotective to a fault when it comes to those he loves. It's a double standard that is equal parts irritating and endearing.

"And she's going to have to fly all the way here *again* when you guys get married."

"I don't think Jonah's even thought about that yet." He's going to lose his mind when he does. My unease grows. "He'll try to convince me to go to Oslo to get married."

"That could be nice."

"No, it could not."

Toby's eyebrow arches in question.

"It's on the other side of the world and I have no roots there."

He considers that for a moment. "Yeah, but Jonah would rock the lederhosen."

I giggle-snort. "Do they wear those there? You know what? It doesn't matter. No wedding in Norway. It's got to be either Toronto or here. My mother is pushing for Toronto." As much as it shocks me, the idea of an Alaskan wedding is sounding more appealing by the day.

Toby scratches his head in thought. "*Or* you could get married now, since Jonah's mom is already here."

I laugh off his joke. "Yeah, right."

But Toby's expression says he isn't kidding this time. "Why not? Your parents will be here, too. My dad could marry you." He nods toward Teddy, fumbling with the screen stand while tugging at the back of his jeans to keep them from falling down. "He got his certification a bunch of years ago when my cousin was getting married. He can legally marry you. All you'd need is the license."

Toby is *actually* serious. "I can't."

"Why not? Who else do you really need?"

"Well, I mean … Diana! She's my maid of honor. I can't get married without her!" I sputter over my answer. While I haven't begun planning our wedding yet, what Toby is suggesting is far from what I had envisioned.

"I'm sure she'd understand, given the health concerns."

"My mother would kill me. She has her heart set on the real deal."

"It'll still be real. Just … simpler." Toby shrugs, his eyes flickering to the engagement ring on my finger, an intricate display of diamonds set in a snowflake design. "Anyway, it's a thought."

"Hey! Enough gabbing, you two!" Muriel claps her hands. "We only have seven hours left before people start showing up."

"*Only* seven more hours of this," Toby murmurs, casting a secretive wink before continuing to adjust the next table.

I dash off to the storage room for the linens, Toby's suggestion lingering in the back of my mind.

"Did you find them?"

I track Muriel's voice to the doorway where she stands next to Roy. A sizeable cardboard box sits in his arms. "Yup." I hold the packages of votive candles in the air as proof. Despite the persistent chill in the community center, rummaging around the cluttered storage room has made my skin feel clammy, and I use this opportunity to brush my forearm against my forehead. "They weren't in the green bins."

Muriel purses her lips, her accusing gaze flipping to Jamie Gill, who oversaw last year's Christmas dinner cleanup and is, in Muriel's own words, "as scattered as an upturned bowl of glitter."

I toss the packages onto one of the rectangular buffet tables—someone *else* can fill and light a hundred and fifty candles because it's almost four P.M. and I have yet to take a break—and stroll over to them. "Hey, Roy."

He grunts, his attention wandering over the hall.

"Looks good in here, huh?" Supersized poinsettias donated from the local garden center mark the doors and Santa's threshold. The centerpieces they've used every year were tacky and dated, so I repurposed the vases and pinecones and added birch branches that Emily and I scavenged from the forest to make chic displays. And, after twenty minutes of begging, I convinced Muriel to let Toby and me string strands of white twinkle lights canopy-style over the dressed tables, creating a cozy ambiance.

We've managed to transform the drab, drafty room into a place primed for a festive party.

I nod toward the box. "Whatcha got there?"

"Somethin' for the auction," he grumbles.

"A *donation* from Roy Donovan?" I can't hide the surprise from my voice, even as I tease. Getting so much as a free egg out of this man is a rarity.

Roy scowls. "Didn't turn out. Was gonna burn it, but I figured I may as well let you guys have it. See if you can make a few bucks."

"What is it?" I lean over to steal a glimpse at a wooden basket nestled inside.

"It's for harvesting the garden," Muriel explains.

I frown. "You were going to burn this? It looks perfect to me."

"The handle's wonky. Here." He thrusts the box toward Muriel. "Gotta get back to milk the goats before it gets too dark." He bolts out with nothing more than a nod my way.

I chase after him, out into the hall. "Hey, Roy, why don't you come back for dinner after you're done with the animals? I know my table has a few extra seats." I would have asked Astrid and Björn to come, but I figured they'll be falling asleep at their table settings by five.

He keeps marching toward the door. "I don't do Christmas."

"But you *do eat*." I temper the annoyance in my tone. "They're serving turkey and roast beef ... and apple pie for dessert." A weakness of Roy's, I learned this past fall when I was experimenting with pastry.

"I've got dinner ready."

"Yeah, canned meat." Eating the same meal seven days a week is bound to make anyone certifiable. "Come on, Roy. You can sit with me. You don't even have to talk, if you don't want to. But you shouldn't be alone."

He snorts. "I've been alone for over thirty years. No reason to change that now."

I can think of one reason. Three, actually. An impulsive urge strikes me. "Hey, Roy?" I clear my voice to steady it. "So, I was thinking ... have you ever given any thought to maybe reaching out to your daughter? Maybe she'd want to hear from you. You never know."

He stops abruptly and spins around. His eyes narrow as he studies me for one ... two ... three long seconds. "You been snoopin' through my things, girl?"

"No." I punctuate that with a firm headshake but have to avert my gaze to the speckled linoleum floor. *Real smooth, Calla.*

Roy is a lot of things, but naïve is not one of them. "Yeah, you have. That's why you're being so pushy all of a sudden, isn't it?"

Shit. There's no point lying. "I saw the Christmas card on your table yesterday and ... I didn't mean to snoop."

"Yes, you did." He stabs the air with his index finger, his face turning beet red with anger. "You're always pokin' around, tryin' to fix things for me. But you can't fix this!" His deep, grating voice ricochets along the narrow hall.

There's no point backing down now. "It seems like she'd *really* like to talk to you, though."

"That's 'cause she don't know me. If she did, she'd figure out pretty quick that I've got nothin' to give her or those two kids."

I frown. "I don't think she was reaching out to you because she wants money, Roy."

"Mind your own business. It ain't got nothin' to do with you!" He slams his palms against the double doors, throwing them open on his rush to exit. "And don't be bringin' over any more goddamn Christmas trees!" he hollers.

I shiver against the gust of frigid air that sweeps in. Or maybe it's because of the layer of ice that's just coated our relationship.

"Haven't seen him that mad in a while. For once, it's not on account of me." Muriel sidles up beside me, her eyes following his wiry body as he stomps to his truck. "So, his daughter's finally wantin' to get to know him."

"I shouldn't have said anything." Jonah's right. Roy is as temperamental as a wild animal. Whatever trust I've earned has disintegrated. An ache swells in my chest with that knowledge.

"Nah." She waves my concern away as if it's a mild inconvenience. "Don't be too bothered by his little tantrum. What Roy wants and what he says he wants are usually two different things."

"Still."

Muriel's lips twist in thought. "Did you get her information?"

I hesitate. "Maybe."

That knowing smile forms. "I don't need to tell you what *I'd* do if *I* had her number."

"I know." She'd be on the phone within the next five minutes, informing Roy's daughter that Roy is a horse's ass, but she should fly up here right away to meet him, anyway. There's no way I'm giving Delyla's number to Muriel. "Let's stick with those wool socks you made him. No need to give Roy another heartache for Christmas." Some say Muriel was at the root of his first one, years ago.

"Don't worry, I won't say a word to him about it. We still got that truce, after all, and I don't need a reason to shoot him over the holidays." She turns to head back to the hall, but then stalls. "You know, me and that old badger go back decades, through all kinds of hardships. And, sure, we've had our disagreements. But I ain't ever seen him as happy as he's been since you've been around. That says somethin'."

I snort. "You call *that* happy?" She heard Roy yelling at me. Hell, everyone in the hall must have heard it.

"Oh, don't buy none of what he's tryin' to sell you. He pretends to enjoy his solitude, but that's all that is. *Pretending,* by a chickenshit who's too afraid to admit that he cares."

A mental image of Roy, sitting in his quiet little cabin alone on Christmas night, hits me. A lump flares in my throat. "I think that makes me even sadder."

"Yeah. For a man who doesn't like pity, he sure draws a lot of it. But enough about Roy for the time being." Muriel checks her watch. "It's after four. Suppose we should dig out those costumes. And I need your help figurin' out what to do with Jessie Winslow's gingerbread house for the silent auction."

I fall in line next to her and, while her legs are far shorter than mine, I need to hustle to keep up. "What's wrong with Jessie's gingerbread house?"

Muriel gives me a look. "I think it's what you people call a 'Pinterest fail.'"

CHAPTER FIVE

Our log home in the woods is a welcome sight when I push through the front door that night. I inhale the medley of comforting scents—the burning wood in the fireplace, fresh evergreen boughs I've trimmed the tables and thresholds with, and the unexpected fragrant spice of gingerbread.

The glow from a table lamp and the lit Christmas tree draws me into the living room and instantly soothes my tired body.

"Hey." I smile at Jonah stretched out on the couch with a novel in his hand.

He breaks his gaze on the page to greet me, and a wide grin splits his handsome face. "So, what did you go by? Sugarplum? Candy Cane?"

I groan. The frumpy elf costume Muriel pulled from a trash bag and instructed me to put on is three sizes too big, torn at the seam, and smells of mothballs. I was too tired to change out of it before heading home.

"Glitter Toes?"

"Shut up."

He shuts his book. "Frosty it is."

"Are Astrid and Björn here … *oh my God*." My mouth gapes as

I take in the disaster in the dimly lit kitchen. Every square inch of counter has a bowl or pot or utensil—or all three, piled high—on it. The sink is full of dirty dishes. I squint at the splatter of white on the ceiling above the island. "Is that icing?" Our kitchen hasn't looked like this since the weekend we moved in and assumed the remnants of Phil and his late wife's thirty-year marriage.

"Yeah, they're upstairs, and she said to leave it. She'll clean everything when she gets up in the morning."

I hope so because I spent a week scrubbing and arranging this place. My mom and Simon arrive tomorrow. "All this for *gingerbread?*"

"She started making some things for Christmas Eve dinner, too."

"Right." Astrid did say she wanted to celebrate, Norwegian style. Apparently "Norwegian style" means trashing my kitchen.

I push the mess—and my annoyance—aside and instead focus on the elaborate multitier house displayed on the dining table. "She *made* this?"

"Yeah. Crazy, huh? She makes them every year. That one's actually pretty plain. Some of the ones she's done in the past, she's submitted to competitions. She's won a few of them."

"You never told me she was an artist." I bend over to inspect the gingerbread house that sits atop a gingerbread base, surrounded by star-shaped gingerbread cookies, stacked from largest to smallest to form evergreen trees. Every edge is trimmed with white royal icing swirls and dots, piped with intricate detail. "She did this all in *one day?*"

"Nah. She baked the pieces back home. Packed them up really well so they wouldn't break on the way here."

I give him a look.

Jonah shrugs. "What can I say? She takes her gingerbread houses seriously."

"This is incredible. Like, I wish she'd come sooner. We could have auctioned this off tonight and made some real cash."

Instead, Muriel made a twenty-dollar pity bid on Jessie's disastrous kit house—which she was most certainly drunk while putting together.

"Did you bid on anything?"

"*Oh.* You've got to see this." I retrieve the garden harvest basket from where I left it by the door and carry it over for Jonah.

He inspects the perfect cuts and skilled craftmanship. "Well made."

"That's because Roy made it."

"*Roy* donated something? What, did Muriel threaten him?"

I laugh. "I know, right? He said the handle was wonky so he couldn't sell it. He was going to burn it."

Jonah tests the handle and then shakes his head. "There's nothing wrong with it. It's solid."

Just like there was nothing wrong with the moose roast Roy claimed was rancid when he thrust it into my hands, and nothing wrong with the bales of hay he said his goats wouldn't eat when he dropped them off for Zeke, and nothing wrong with the firewood he chopped and stacked outside the cabin, claiming the logs wouldn't burn right at his place.

Jonah sets the garden basket on the floor beside the couch. "So, how was your day?"

I flop on the couch beside him. "Long. Exhausting. But successful, I guess—Ah!" I squeal as Jonah grabs hold of my ankles and pulls my legs across his lap.

And then I let out a low groan of delight as he begins rubbing my sore feet.

"*Oh,* Marie says hi."

"Muriel suckered her into helping out, too?"

"No. She was just there in the morning to drop off an auction prize. A bunch of pet food and toys. And, hey, *I* didn't get *suckered* into anything. Muriel highlighted how my talents and contributions have proven invaluable to the town, and so I graciously offered my services."

Jonah smirks. "What'd she have you do today?"

"You mean, what *didn't* she have me do." I yank off my elf's hat and settle my head back against the throw pillow. Jonah's skilled thumbs work magic on my heels as I describe a day of rooting through dusty storage boxes, climbing a wobbly ladder a dozen times to string lights, and corralling the youngest and most impressionable of Trapper's Crossing's children as they scampered to Santa Teddy's lap to relay urgent, last-minute requests.

"The kid *peed* on him?"

"*Two* kids peed on him," I correct. "But this one was the first kid of the night, and he must have had a full bladder." A chubby-cheeked, three-year-old boy named Thomas who whispered about wanting a train set by the same name while staring at Teddy's bushy white beard, mesmerized.

And then he let loose.

I didn't realize what was happening until Teddy, ever the jovial one, peered down at the small puddle forming by his feet.

"Teddy excused himself and went to the back room to change his pants. They have a spare because apparently, he gets peed on *every* year."

Jonah's head falls back in a burst of deep laughter.

"Shhh! You'll wake them up!" I warn, nudging his thigh with my toes, but I'm giggling, too.

"Remind me to *never* agree to do anything like that."

"I thought you wanted kids," I mock.

"Not to *piss* on me."

"That's what they do. They pee and vomit on you, and they smear their poop *all over* the walls like it's finger paint." According to Sharon, anyway. I've kept in touch with the old receptionist from Alaska Wild over email. She and Max are enjoying their time in Portland with baby Thor, though she says Max is itching to come back.

"Fine. *My* kids can do that on me. Other kids can do that on someone else."

I smile. Hearing Jonah talk about kids and being a parent doesn't spark the same tension it used to, back when we were charging headfirst into this relationship without pause. In fact, it no longer fazes me. Sometimes I find myself wondering how many we'll end up having, what they'll be, and who they'll take after more. Will they have my hair? Jonah's eyes?

Will Jonah's son inherit those same adorable dimples that used to hide behind that unruly beard of his?

His stubbornness?

His love of flying?

Jonah catches me staring at him. A curious look flickers across his face. "What?"

"Nothing." The truth is, if we had a repeat of this past summer and the pregnancy test turned out positive rather than a scare, I don't think I'd be so fearful of the idea. At the same time, I'm not ready to share Jonah's undivided attention just yet. "What happened here? Besides the epic disaster in the kitchen."

"Not much. Came home around one, moved them over, we hung out, ate dinner."

"No more fighting with Björn?"

"He had a four-hour nap, woke up in time for my mom to serve him his dinner, and then he went back to bed an hour ago. I barely saw him." Jonah smirks. "Let's hope jet lag messes with him until he leaves."

Not likely, but a sleepy Björn might make for a more pleasant Christmas under this roof.

Jonah peels off my sock and wraps his large hands around my foot so I don't feel the chill. "My mom brought up the wedding. Asked if we've thought about a date yet."

"Yeah, she mentioned it this morning, too." "With her health the way it is, I don't want her flying back and forth for our wedding."

I knew that was coming. "What did she say about it?"

"It doesn't matter what she says. She'll still fly, even if she shouldn't. But *I'm* not good with it."

"I know." And, as much as Jonah jokes about running off and eloping, I know he would want his mother there. "What do you want to do, then?" I feel like I already know where this conversation is heading, and a tiny, selfish part of me wants to resist.

Jonah bites his lip in thought, watching me carefully. "I was thinking—"

"You are *not* wearing lederhosen," I blurt.

He frowns. "*What*? Why would I wear those?"

"Are you about to suggest we get married in Oslo?"

"Fuck. *No*." He shakes his head to emphasize that. "I was gonna ask if you'd consider getting married now, while they're here."

I groan. "Not you, too."

His frown deepens. "What do you mean?"

"Toby and I were talking about your mom and her health issues, and he said we should do it now and Teddy could officiate."

"Teddy?"

"Yeah. Apparently, he's certified to officiate over weddings."

Jonah snorts with disbelief, but then his brow furrows in serious thought.

I know that look taking over his face. It's one of determination.

"No." I shake my head.

Jonah grasps my calves, drags my body over, and pulls me up to straddle his lap. His arms curl around my body. "Why not?" His blue eyes twinkle with earnestness.

I laugh. "Because it's too rushed, and because Diana's not here, and because ... it's too rushed!" All the obstacles that have cycled through my mind spill out. "I don't want to just sign a paper and be married! That's not a memorable day for us!"

"So, then, we make it memorable." There's a hint of challenge in his voice.

"Oh, come on! In a week? *How*? Things take *forever* up here on a regular day, and it's the Christmas holidays, *and* there's a massive winter storm coming that's probably going to knock out power for days. And, I mean, good luck getting any flowers or a decent dress or a caterer. And what about a honeymoon—"

"Okay. Whoa. Relax. It was just an idea." Jonah lifts his hands in the air in a sign of surrender. "I'm not gonna pressure you to marry me."

"I *am* marrying you. Remember?" I wave my hand to show off my diamond ring.

He sighs, and I can tell something is weighing on him.

"What is it?"

"Honestly? You've had that ring for four months now. I guess I figured you'd be itching to make some plans, but you don't seem to be in any rush." His jaw tenses. "I'm beginning to wonder if you have doubts."

"Um ... we've been kind of busy. Remember, there was that thing about you crashing your plane and almost *dying*, and then we were renovating the cabin, and I was neck-deep in Winter Carnival planning and getting ready for Christmas."

"I know, I just—"

I collect his face in my palms, forcing his gaze to mine. "I have *never* been more sure of anything than I am of wanting to marry you," I say slowly, clearly, to ensure he hears it.

"Then why does it seem like you keep avoiding making any decisions?" he asks softly, but there's the slightest touch of something in his voice. Accusation, maybe. Hurt, possibly.

"I'm not. I ..." My voice drifts. Does it really seem like that? If I am avoiding setting a date, it's not for any doubts I have about Jonah. "Maybe I'm just having a hard time deciding where it should be. I mean, you know my mom is hell-bent on Toronto. And my whole life was back there until this year, and now so much of it is *here*, but that's still my past. My family, my friends. None of those people are going to fly all the way here to see me get married."

Maybe that's what I'm having a hard time with. Not sharing one of the biggest days of my life with the people who know me best. "It's just ... I don't know how I could pull it off in a meaningful way. Believe me, I thought about it." All afternoon, I dwelled on it, weighing the pros and cons. "And don't get me started on dealing with my mother."

"Susan's had *two* weddings of her own," Jonah says dryly.

"I know. And I don't know why I'm putting so much stock into her opinion here." Other than that she's my mother and I feel like I've already taken something away from her by moving across the continent.

"You know that none of that stuff—the flowers, the cake, whatever else there is—none of it matters to me." He scoops my palm and brings it to his mouth for a kiss, his beard tickling my skin. "But I know it matters to you."

"We'll figure something out that works for everyone," I promise. I just don't know what that looks like yet.

Reaching behind, he pulls me forward, flush against his body. "You have to admit, it would have been perfect, though."

"How so?"

"Christmas wedding in Alaska." He dips his face into the crook of my neck. I close my eyes and revel in his lips against my throat and the feel of him growing hard against the apex of my thighs. "Me, marrying Frosty the Elf with Santa officiating."

I snort.

"You wouldn't even need a dress when you've got *this*."

"Are you kidding? I'm burning this costume in the fireplace tonight. Seriously. And I'm going to round up all the others tomorrow, and burn them, too. I'll order new ones for next year."

"I think it's cute." He inhales deeply. And pauses. "Is that you that smells like mothballs?"

"See? Ugh!" I peel off the felt potato sack and toss it next to the fireplace, leaving me in the red-and-green-striped pants and the black Lycra top I wore underneath.

Jonah makes a sound, his excited eyes roaming the material that's stretched across my chest like a second skin. "You still smell." He tugs on my shirt.

"Not *here*!" I hiss, nodding toward the upstairs where Astrid and Björn are tucked away.

"Why not? They took sleeping pills. They'll be dead to the world until at least four. Come on, arms up."

I hesitate but then reach over to turn off the table lamp, leaving us in darkness save for the white lights on the tree, the fire, and a small over-stove light in the kitchen. I lift my aching arms high above my head, allowing him easy access to strip my shirt off me. Warmth from the fire radiates against my back, but there's still a chill in the air, made all the more obvious when he unfastens the hook of my bra.

"Jonah," I admonish softly, but the mood in the room is shifting quickly, his hands eagerly slipping over my bared chest. Heat courses through my body beneath his skilled touch.

I don't utter another word of complaint as I shift and shimmy to help him work off my striped pants.

"Cute," he whispers, noting the mistletoe print on my panties before also sliding them off. That we're not alone in the house seems to goad us into moving swiftly, peeling off his shirt, pushing his sweatpants and boxers down his thighs. His erection stands at attention. "Something's missing." He looks around. "Oh, yeah." Grabbing the elf hat, he positions it on my head. "There. Perfect."

My mouth is on his, my tongue teasing the seam of his lips as he reaches down between us to grip and line himself up, when the bottom step creaks.

With a startled gasp, I peel away from Jonah's mouth and look over to find a shirtless Björn ambling toward the kitchen, his eyes half-closed, his steps heavy with sleep.

Fumbling for the wool blanket stretched across the back of the couch, I quickly wrap it around our naked bodies, and then offer Jonah a scathing glare.

Jonah tips his head back to watch his stepfather dig a glass out of the cupboard and go to the fridge to fill it with water from the Brita. "I don't think he saw us," he whispers, a hint of amusement in his voice as we huddle on the couch, naked other than the blanket, and in a compromising position.

I don't think Björn is even fully awake. He casually scratches his round belly as he gulps a full glass of water. He then fills it up again and shuts the fridge, muttering something in Norwegian as he wanders back toward the stairs.

I hold my breath.

Just before he takes that first step, he turns to the couch and sees us there, silently watching him, and there is no way a lucid adult would *not* be able to put two and two together and realize what he interrupted.

"Nice hat," he mutters and then eases back upstairs, using the rail to help him.

My cheeks burn with mortification. "I can't believe that happened." Did he see us on his way down and pretend that he didn't? Did he know we were here, naked, the whole time and decide the least awkward handling of the situation would be to ignore us?

What *exactly* did Björn see?

Jonah lets out a heavy sigh of relief that I don't feel at the moment. "Where were we?"

"Going to shower." I climb off Jonah's lap, taking the blanket with me to wrap around my nude body.

"Fucking Björn," I hear Jonah grumble as I scamper up the steps.

CHAPTER SIX

"You know, when I was a kid, we had a golden retriever who waited at the window for my mom to come home," Jonah notes.

I cast a glare over my shoulder and catch Astrid delivering a soft whack against his biceps before she moves her game piece. Along with a gingerbread house—what she keeps calling the *pepperkake*—Astrid brought a suitcase full of housewarming gifts, including an advent candle that is burning in the corner of the living room, an ugly little Christmas gnome that is supposed to bring good luck and is sitting next to Ethel's raven and goose-wife carving, and several jars of edible things for Christmas Eve that I can't identify and most certainly won't eat.

But what excited Jonah most was the Swords and Shields board game that he and Astrid are facing off at now. It's the same one they used to spend hours playing when he was young.

"Come on. Why don't you sit down?" Jonah pats the space on the couch beside him. Not too far over, Björn snores softly in the reclining chair he seems to have claimed as his own. He hasn't made any reference to last night's intrusion, and I can't decide if it's because he wasn't aware what he'd walked in on or if even Björn has an ounce of tact.

"They were supposed to be here forty-five minutes ago, and she's not responding to any of my texts." It's dark. Far darker than anything they're used to driving around Toronto's brightly lit streets.

"Her phone probably died."

"So then she'd used Simon's phone."

"Maybe his died, too."

"Simon travels with battery packs."

Jonah pauses in his move to give me an exasperated look. "I don't know what to tell you, except they'll be here. It's a two-hour drive from Anchorage, it's snowing, and they don't know where they're going, so they'll be driving slow, but they'll be here, Calla."

I refocus my attention out the window, to the pitch-dark broken only by the white twinkle lights we stung around the porch. It'll be a year tomorrow since Mom and Simon dropped me off at Pearson with my one-way ticket in hand. Sure, we talk and text regularly, and FaceTime often enough, but a screen can't replace sitting across from real-life Simon while he sips his tea and doles out wisdom, and no matter how many times I inhale, I'll never catch a whiff of my mother's floral perfume through the phone line.

I knew I'd miss them when I left.

I didn't realize how much.

Finally, I spot the dull beam of light, followed by two glowing orbs slowly moving up our driveway. My squeal awakens a dozing Björn as I rush through the living room to the door, throw on my bulky coat and boots, and charge outside. I slip and nearly wipe out on the snowy path as I rush to where the SUV comes to a stop.

"You would *not believe* the time we had at the rental place," my mother exclaims in a flurry, sliding out of the passenger seat. "They tried to sell us an upgrade, and when we said we didn't need an upgrade, they tried to downgrade us to a minivan—a minivan! On these roads!—because they didn't have the SUV we requested. Can you believe that? Oh my gosh, I'm tired. Come here." Mom ropes her arms around my neck and pulls me in tight to her. "I've missed you *so* much."

"I've missed you, too." I return the long embrace, exhaling at the first hint of her perfume. It's a bit like the nostalgia of coming home. "Looks like it all worked out, though?"

"Oh, *this*?" She waves a gloved hand at the BMW. "Well, yes, I suggested that if they can't accommodate our reservation, they'd better give us the next best thing for the same price."

"Your mother has a funny way of 'suggesting' things." Simon pulls his knit hat over his balding head as he rounds the hood of the SUV. "I'm surprised we didn't leave there in handcuffs. No matter, though. We're here now."

I dive into Simon's lanky body, my eyes burning with overwhelming joy at having them both here after waiting so long.

The front door creaks open and Jonah climbs down the front stairs without a coat, his boots unlaced. "Susan, Simon, good to see you again." He envelops my mother in a hug that makes her laugh with surprise and then reaches for Simon's hand to give it a firm shake. "We're happy you made it."

"I'm used to more streetlights at night. I had my eyes peeled for a moose." Simon pops the trunk.

"You'll see one around here in the morning. Here, I got 'em."

"They're heavy," he warns. "Susan packed."

Jonah hauls two of the three suitcases out. "How's this thing in snow, anyway? Better than Calla's Jeep, I'm guessing?"

My head falls back with a groan.

"What's wrong with Calla's Jeep?" My mother frowns at it.

"*Nothing* is wrong with it. He wants me in a tank." I shoot an exasperated look at Jonah. He's relentless.

"At least you wouldn't be able to drive too fast in that." He smirks on his way past me and up the path, effortlessly carrying the two cases by the handles, one in each hand.

"My future son-in-law certainly is strong," Mom murmurs, appreciation in her voice.

Simon grunts as he struggles to heave the last suitcase out of the SUV. "Obviously, he took the *much* lighter ones."

I wake to a grating sound, followed by silence, and then again that noisy rattle for another moment before more silence. I smile. Simon is attempting to grind fresh coffee beans without disturbing the entire household. It's what he does whenever he forgets to prepare them the night before.

I'm eager to get to the kitchen and enjoy my first Simon-served latte in a year. I've been anticipating this moment for months.

Beside me, Jonah stirs momentarily at the pulsing sound but then settles again. It's almost nine A.M. He's always up by now, stoking the fire and checking the weather reports for the day. But I guess the last week of poor sleep in anticipation of everyone's arrival has finally caught up to him.

The nightstand clock casts just enough light that I can make out the lines of his handsome face, peacefully boyish in sleep. I study it now, though I've long since memorized every detail of it —the mannish cut of his jawline, the curve of the scar across his forehead, the new scar above his eyebrow, the long fringe of lashes a shade darker than his ash-blond hair, the crinkle lines at the corners of his eyes that seem more prominent now than they were when we first met. They only add to his attractiveness.

What will Jonah look like in five? Ten? Twenty years from now?

Still handsome, I'm sure. Probably more so, regardless of the wrinkles and scars that he'll earn, chasing children on the ground and miles in the air.

"I can feel you staring at me," Jonah suddenly croaks, a second before his eyelid cracks open. "Why are you staring at me?"

"Because you're *so pretty*."

With a deep groan, he shifts to climb on top of me, fitting his body between my thighs. One hand reaches down to tug my pajama bottoms off.

"Simon is *right below* us!" I whisper harshly. They probably all are. They're all suffering from jet lag.

"Then don't scream like you usually do." Jonah slides off his boxer briefs. His skin is hot against mine as he pushes inside me without any foreplay. Neither of us seems to need it this morning, though.

The bed creaks noisily as his hips begin moving.

"Shhh!" I scold, but I can't help the giggle that escapes.

Jonah thrusts harder in answer, and I press my mouth against his shoulder to muffle my moan.

Below us, the coffee grinder whirrs. This time, it keeps going.

The sun has crested the horizon and is pouring through our bay window, casting our house in a warm morning glow, when I reach the landing—well over an hour later than I intended when I first woke up.

"... I *always* recommend ranunculus and peonies. They're timeless."

"Hmm. Yes, you are right. Those are lovely."

Mom and Astrid are sitting side by side at the kitchen counter, surrounded by a medley of scattered wedding magazines. They're both dressed for the day, Astrid in a crisp white button-down top and jeans, my mother in a stylish cranberry-colored cable-knit sweater and black leggings. While I wouldn't call them opposites, Astrid has a much more simplistic style.

"Oh, good morning, honey! Hope you slept well," Mom offers,

sharing a secretive, amused look with Astrid from above the rim of her latest reading glasses—she updates her frames each spring—before refocusing on her magazine.

My cheeks flush. At least they seem to be getting along. "Looks like it's going to be a nice day."

"Indeed it does!" Simon echoes, pausing momentarily in his task at the stove to flash me a smile. "Give me a sec and I'll whip you up a latte."

I frown. "You sure you can manage it?" I can't remember the last time I saw Simon cook anything beyond instant mashed potatoes. Yet, every burner is occupied with a pan or pot, the smell of bacon permeating the air. He's even donned one of my Christmas aprons over his standard sweater-vest-and-slacks outfit.

"Of course! Low and slow is the ticket." Simon gives the hash browns a swirl with a wooden spoon before shaking off his oven mitts.

"Since you've moved out, Simon has rediscovered his passion for cooking," my mom informs me through a sip of her frothy beverage, adding dryly, "He's also on his *third* cup of coffee this morning."

"Third," I echo, my eyebrows arching. His limit has always been one, and Simon's nothing if not a creature of habit. "That explains a lot."

"I'll have another. Astrid," Björn calls from his spot in the recliner, his attention riveted on the novel in his meaty grasp. He squints against the blinding sun while holding out his ceramic mug, as if expecting her to retrieve it.

Astrid doesn't hesitate, shifting to leave her stool.

But I'm already on my feet and closer. "I've got it." I veer toward the idle man in my living room.

Björn looks up from his page and appears momentarily startled to see me. "Oh. Okay. Black, please."

"Hmm-hmm." I saunter toward the coffee pot.

"What's wrong, your legs don't work, Björn?" Jonah casually throws out on his way down the stairs, fresh from his shower. There's no bite to his tone, but I give him a warning look, anyway.

"Yeah, yeah," he murmurs, smoothing an affectionate hand across the small of my back as he passes me, heading for Astrid. He leans down to drop a quick kiss on her forehead. "Better night of sleep, Mom?"

She beams as she peers up at him. "Yes. The twin beds are nice. I don't have to deal with his tossing and turning."

"And how about you two?" He looks between Simon and my mother, his eyebrows raised in question.

"Like a baby on Ambien," my mother muses, holding up her magazine to show me a chic barn decked out in white lights and floral arrangements. "What do you think about this venue, Calla? It's a vineyard in the County. That's an up-and-coming wine region in Ontario," she adds for Jonah's and Astrid's benefit, her green eyes flittering between them. "They only allow a few weddings a year, but I know the owners. I'll bet if I contacted them, they would be more than happy to accommodate you two."

"We haven't decided where we're getting married yet," I remind her as calmly as I can. I was hoping to at least have my coffee in hand before she started in on this. "And the County is *two hours* outside of Toronto. Everyone would have to travel there."

"Well, yes, I'm aware, but it's much easier than your family and friends flying to *Alaska*, honey." She's using that coaxing tone, the one she pulls out when she's trying to convince me to see that she's right.

Simon clears his throat.

"Of course, there's Jonah's family to think of, too," she rushes to add, looking to Astrid. "How much family do you have in Norway?"

"Oh, well …" Astrid slides off her black-rimmed reading

glasses. "There is my one brother, Arne, and his wife and daughters, and my other brother, Oddvar. He has three children and four grandchildren. No, *five* grandchildren now. And there's my one surviving uncle on my mother's side ..."

She rhymes off names as I top Björn's mug with fresh black coffee and then hold out the pot, offering to fill Jonah's mug for him.

"Great. A bunch of strangers at our wedding," Jonah murmurs under his breath, loud enough for only me to hear.

"They're not *all* strangers. You know Björn's kids," I tease, waiting for his scowl.

It comes almost immediately while taking his first sip.

"I've mentioned this to Calla before but, with guests spread out from Alaska to Norway, it would make *far* more sense to choose a central location for the wedding. Like Toronto. Wouldn't you agree?"

Astrid's brow furrows. "I suppose so."

"See, kids?" Mom smiles triumphantly.

"Mom ..." I warn. She's pushing too hard.

"*Or* they could get married in Oslo," Astrid counters, flipping through pages of wedding dresses. "Right, vennen?" I note the edge of challenge in her tone. Is she suggesting this because it's what she'd prefer, or because she suddenly feels the need to have an equal voice in her only son's wedding?

"I don't think ..." My mom's brow furrows. She wasn't expecting that answer. "Well, I guess it'll be easier to figure out once they choose a date and we draft a guest list. See where the majority of people are located. Agreed?"

Astrid nods slowly. "That sounds prudent."

I meet Jonah's gaze and find him smirking. We both know that no matter how many names Astrid produces, my mother will double that number and they'll all be Toronto based.

And all of this is a moot point because neither of them is deciding where Jonah and I are getting married!

"You know, there's a way to avoid *all* this," he reminds me. He must see the ire in my eyes.

"It's tempting at the moment," I admit.

"What's tempting?" my mother asks.

"Nothing," Jonah and I say in unison.

Simon holds out an extra crispy slice of bacon with a set of tongs for me. "I think you and Jonah should decide what's best for you, and we will help make that happen. Right, Susan?"

If he feels her scathing glare at his back, he ignores it, smiling wide at us.

"Thank you—hey!" I squeal as Jonah intercepts the piece. I snatch it from his grasp with a glower, earning his playful grin.

"Is my coffee ready?" Björn hollers from the living room.

That playful grin evaporates instantly. Jonah opens his mouth —no doubt to offer a confrontational retort.

I shove the slice of bacon into his mouth to shut him up, capping it off with a finger waggle of warning.

"Here, I'll take that." Astrid holds out her hands to collect Björn's mug from me.

"Calla, where did you say those eggs were?" Simon holds out an open carton with only one egg inside.

"Bottom shelf. I bought two dozen on Friday."

"Oh, I used those," Astrid says, setting Björn's coffee on the table beside him before patting his shoulder with affection.

"*All* of them?"

"Well, yes. The *Kvæfjordkake* and *Karamellpudding* alone take a dozen eggs. The *risengrynsgrøt* doesn't have any, but then there's the …" Astrid names several dishes I can't interpret, leaving Simon to scratch his chin as he studies the pans on the stove and the lonely egg.

I sigh. "I'll run over to Roy's and see if I can get a few more from him."

"I don't want you to go to all that trouble—"

"It's just down the road. Ten minutes at most. No big deal."

Normally, it wouldn't be. Who knows what kind of reception I'll get after our fight the other night.

"If you're sure."

"That we can't have Simon's world-famous, English-style eggs-and-bacon breakfast without eggs?" I head for the coat hooks and slip on my winter jacket. "Besides, I have to drop off Roy's Christmas gifts to him."

"You want me to come with you?" Jonah offers.

I can't tell if he's offering because he wants to get away from all the wedding pressure or because he knows I'm nervous about Roy. Either way, it's best if I approach the curmudgeon on my own. "I'm good."

I'm tugging on my winter hat when the side door creaks open and Muriel plows through, stomping her heavy boots on the doormat. She must have driven her truck in because I didn't hear an engine approach.

"Morning, all!" She saunters in, bringing a draft of cold air with her.

I make quick introductions.

"Oh, I've heard plenty about *all* of you. Your kids have been counting down the days to have you here." Muriel's shrewd gaze halts on the gingerbread house displayed in the middle of the dining table. "Would you look at that." She marches over to get a closer view, leaving snowy footprints across the floor. We've had words about her bad habit of tracking mud and snow across our hardwood floors. She's gotten better about it. Most of the time. "Calla said you were busy baking the other day, Astrid?"

Astrid smiles. "Yes. It is a passion of mine."

"Too bad we didn't have that for the auction, right?" I step into my boots.

"I don't know. I think people'd feel guilty eatin' this thing." After another appraising look, Muriel shifts her attention back to me. "Where you off to?"

"Roy's. We ran out of eggs and Simon's cooking breakfast."

"And you are more than welcome to join us," Simon offers cordially.

Muriel waves him off. "That's kind of you, but I ate hours ago. I can't stay. I just wanted to bring this moose roast over." She holds up the bulky, butcher-paper-wrapped package from under her arm. "Figured you folks probably don't get moose too often and you might enjoy it one night for dinner."

Jonah's all smiles as he retrieves it from her. "You know *I* will. Thanks."

Muriel dips her head. "That's what neighbors do, isn't it? We take care of each other."

Astrid smiles warmly, watching the exchange. "Did you get that during this year's hunt, Muriel?"

"Me? No. I don't go moose hunting much anymore. Not since ..." Her voice trails with her stern frown, and I know she's thinking about her missing son. "No, this is from my cousin Eddie. He must have put his name in that lottery ten ... fifteen years ago. I told him he'd never get the call but a couple weeks ago, he got the call and made a liar out of me. A fourteen-hundred-pound bull!" She shakes her head. "How that driver walked away from that wreck, I'll never know."

My mother frowns at the package in Jonah's hand. "What do you mean? Is that—"

"Roadkill. We don't waste good meat in Alaska. It all tastes the same. Don't matter if it's a bullet or a grill that took it down, does it?" If Muriel notices the disgust flitter across my mother's face, she ignores it, turning her attention to me. "I heard you want Teddy to perform your wedding ceremony. Now, he's more than happy to do it, no problem there, but if you want it done a hundred percent legal, you need to get down to the courthouse to apply for the marriage license today, because they make you wait three business days before they'll issue it."

I'm momentarily stunned. I didn't expect to be blindsided like this. "I didn't—"

"And with Christmas, everything's going to be all messed up. 'Course, you can go through the motions while everyone's here and then he'll sign the license after the fact, if you can't get it before they all have to fly home."

I'm going to kill Toby.

"Calla? What *on earth* is she talking about?"

I face my wide-eyed mother who looks like she blinked and suddenly found herself in a stranger's house. On another planet. "There was a *suggestion* made that we get married while you're all here, to make it easier on everyone."

"But you're not considering it, are you?" Her jaw drops. "Oh my God, you're pregnant, aren't you?"

"Hell, I wish." Jonah barks with laughter.

"Jonah!" Astrid admonishes softly, but her lips curl with a smile as if she's struggling to hide her amusement.

"But you *can't* get married before we leave. That's ... that's ... absurd. I mean, where will I find flowers for your bouquet? And a dress! In a *week*? Good luck! And what about the venue?"

"Already checked and the community center is available," Muriel chirps, thinking she's being helpful. "You could reuse all the decorations from Saturday night, too. I'll tell Jamie to leave it up."

"The *community center*!" My mother's laugh is bordering on hysterical now. "Okay. Let's say for a moment that we go with that. Who's going to do the catering?"

"I'm sure I could get another roast or two out of Eddie," Muriel counters, serious.

"So, my daughter will be serving *roadkill* to her wedding guests."

"She's just trying to help," I snap, not appreciating the caustic tone my mother is taking with Muriel. "And this is *my* wedding, Mom! Not yours!"

But she's barely listening, too wrapped up in her own head. "What does it matter. You won't have any guests. Who could attend? This is crazy!" She looks first to Simon, then to Astrid. "Right? Our only children, *eloping* in some sort of backwoods Hee Haw celebration?"

Astrid shrugs. "I've always preferred a simple, low-key affair. And it's far more practical financially. Right, Björn?"

"Huh?" He peels his attention from his book to peer at his wife. "I'll have mine fried. I think they call it sunny-side up?"

"Way to stay on brand." Jonah shakes his head at his stepfather. "She's not a waitress asking for your fucking egg order."

Björn scowls first at Jonah, then at his wife. "Some mouth on that son of yours, Astrid. If Karl or Ivar spoke to me like that ..." His words drift, as if he need not say more.

"You'd *what,* Björn?" Jonah questions, a taunting gleam in his cold blue eyes. "What would *you do,* huh? Something that required you to get off your lazy ass?"

Björn utters something in Norwegian. He tosses his novel onto the side table, narrowly missing the full cup of coffee just delivered, and stands with surprising speed to face Jonah. "I was the reigning arm wrestling champion for *six years,* you pompous little shit!" He yanks up his shirt sleeves to show off substantial forearms.

"I *like* taking care of my husband, Jonah! Now, *both* of you. Stop this!" Astrid explodes, throwing her arms in the air as if to say "enough." Her hand inadvertently catches the corner of her coffee mug. It topples over and hits the floor, the coffee splashing, the ceramic shattering.

While that commotion is happening, my mother has cast her reading glasses onto the pile of magazines. "Simon, would you talk some sense into *our daughter*? You're the only one she seems to listen to."

She pulled out the "our daughter" card.

Simon's brow furrows, and I know he's choosing his words wisely before he dares utter them, because there is no rationalizing with my mother when she's this emotional.

Muriel tracks back to join me in the hall, watching the flurry of anger unfold. "Bit of a can of worms I might have opened there, huh?"

"You think?" I grab my mittens and keys, and head out the door.

CHAPTER SEVEN

This time when I roll up to Roy's cabin, he emerges from the barn, shutting the door tightly behind him.

I take my time, pausing to scratch Oscar behind the ear and give Gus a pat. Really, I just need another moment to gather the courage I wasn't able to find on the ride here, too busy battling this rising dread that I've finally pushed Roy too far.

"What do you want?" he calls out in his typical gruff style, his arms folded across his chest. He's in his usual outfit—a faded, forest-green, quilted plaid jacket and worn jeans, dusted in wood shavings. I'm not sure they've ever been washed. There's no washer or dryer anywhere on this property, and of the hand-washed things I've seen on the drying rack or clothesline, they've never been included.

There's no point in attempting small talk, not that Roy's ever been for it. "Jonah's mom used all my eggs and didn't tell me, and Simon's in the middle of making breakfast. I was hoping I could grab a half dozen from you." I brace myself for him to bark that he's not a damn grocery store, to get the hell off his property, and out of his life once and for all.

"There's a full carton inside." He waves a hand toward his cabin, a signal that I should go and get them myself.

"Oh. Okay. I'll just …" I begin moving for the front door before he can change his mind.

"Did that garden basket fetch any money for the auction?" he hollers after me, stalling my feet.

"Yeah." I hesitate. "Some might say *too* much. You know, because of that faulty handle."

The corner of his mouth twitches. "How are things going over at your place, with the big meet and greet and all that?"

He's actually making an effort to have a conversation. That's a good sign. "Well …" I find myself wandering back closer. "My mom thinks Jonah and I are having a shotgun wedding next week and serving everyone roadkill at the reception, so she's having a coronary, and I wouldn't be surprised if Björn and Jonah are arm wrestling when I get back." Agnes and Mabel arrive today, and it's a blessing they're staying in the cabin across the lake. At least they have somewhere to escape.

Which reminds me—I need to get out there to prepare it. George and Bobbie said they'd be dropping them off around one, on their way to their cabin up near Fairbanks.

Roy's brow pinches with curious amusement. "And why does your mother think you two are getting married next week?"

"Because Muriel told everyone that we are." I explain Astrid's health condition and Toby's suggestion, in as few words as possible because Roy gets impatient with too many details.

By the time I'm done, he's shaking his head. "The day that woman stops meddling in people's lives is the day she stops breathing."

"She meant well," I defend half-heartedly. "And Astrid probably shouldn't be flying back and forth from Oslo like this. It *is* risky. I'd feel terrible if something happened to her." A reality that's weighing more on me as time passes. "It's just not what I was picturing for myself. It's definitely not what my mother pictured."

Roy leans back against the barn's frame and folds his arms across his chest. "So, you gonna go through with it next week, then?"

"I don't know?" Without much thought, I add, "Should I?"

Roy's bushy eyebrows pop with a flash of surprise. "You askin' *me*? For *wedding* advice?"

"I don't know. Sure." I chuckle. "Why not?" Roy was the first one to find out about our engagement, before my mom and Simon, even before Diana. He was the first to offer congratulations.

And, of all the people who waited with me for news of Jonah's whereabouts on that dreaded night, it was Roy who I found myself leaning on for support.

"You must be lost, then." His thoughts seem to wander as his gaze drifts over the tidy woodpiles beside his truck. "Nicole's parents never wanted her to marry me. At first, they refused to pay for the wedding, but when they realized she was hellbent on doin' it no matter what, even if it meant standin' in front of a judge with a stranger to sign on the witness line, they changed their tune. They gave their daughter the wedding she deserved, even if it was to a guy who didn't deserve her." He drops his eyes to his work boots. "All that money they poured into that fancy affair, and what did it get her? Not happiness, I can tell you that much. At least not with me." He snorts. "Jim … that was the guy. I knew she'd end up back with him."

"She did get a beautiful daughter because of you," I remind him gently. "And then two grandchildren."

He glowers, pulling away from his relaxed stance. "I don't give a shit what other people want, and you shouldn't, either. Marry Jonah while you're standin' in an empty barn wearin' your woolens and surrounded by goat shit, or marry him next year in some big, expensive dog-and-pony show with a bunch of strangers lookin' on. It shouldn't matter to anyone who means anything to you. It sure as hell won't make a stitch of difference to your marriage, 'specially not when the 'for better or worse' hits those 'worse' parts." He reaches for the barn-door handle. "And, for what it's worth, if anyone could pull a wedding out of their ass in a week and make it not suck, it'd be you."

I smile. "I'll take that as a compliment."

"Take it however you want." The barn door rolls open with his tug.

"Hey, why don't you come for dinner tonight?"

"And deal with that shit show you got goin' on over there? No, thanks." The door slides shut with a soft thud behind him.

I take this opportunity to grab the wrapped gifts from my back seat. Inside Roy's cabin, I set them on the floor beside the trunk where the Christmas tree still sits, despite Roy's vehement complaints. Only now, the card from Delyla is propped next to it, and tucked in the corner of the old framed picture of Nicole and Delyla is the four-by-six of her and her children.

"And yet you're not going to call her, are you, you old bugger?" I shake my head as I collect the dozen eggs from the counter where Roy said they'd be.

I take my time on Roy's lengthy driveway and then the road, not in a rush to return to whatever mess is waiting for me. But the entire ride, I'm thinking about Roy and the daughter he won't contact, no matter how badly I suspect he wants to.

I spot the blue snowmachine parked at the hangar when I coast up our driveway. Jonah must have escaped "that shit show" as Roy so aptly described it. As much as I need to get these eggs back to Simon, I divert from my path.

Inside, I find Jonah rifling through the emergency kit stored in Archie. He looks up at the sound of the door slamming shut. "Roy give you some eggs?"

"A dozen."

"Should be enough."

I shudder against the chilly air. Even with the heating system in place, it's never truly warm in here. Jonah is accustomed and unbothered by it. I am not. "What are you doing?"

"Replacing all the granola bars I had in here. I was hungry the other day, so I pulled one out and it tasted like cardboard."

I close the distance and rest my cheek against his shoulder. "What happened after I left?"

"You mean after you abandoned me?" He smirks as he tosses two stale bars into the nearby trash bin before pivoting to lean against the table, facing me. "Let's see … Björn started chirping at me in Norwegian because he knows it pisses me off, so I told him I'd be more than happy to drive him back to the airport. My mother told me to stop being an asshole. I probably deserved that."

"And what about *my* mom?"

Jonah chuckles. "Muriel promised her that the plumbing issue in the community center usually doesn't act up in extremely cold weather, and that everyone would be more than willing to bring food if we held the reception there."

"Oh my God. A potluck wedding in a community center." I groan. "So basically my mother's worst nightmare."

"Sounds pretty good if you ask me, but that vein on her forehead was pulsing. That's when I left."

I fall against Jonah's broad chest, welcoming his comforting arms around me. "Why did Muriel have to do that?"

"It's not her fault, and none of this is a surprise. We knew we were going to get the gears about setting a date from both sides, and that your mother would be pushing hard for a wedding in Toronto."

I inhale the familiar scent of Jonah—spearmint gum and woodsy soap—as I think about Roy's words. "What do *you* want to do, Jonah?"

His chest heaves with his sigh. "I'll do *whatever* you want—"

"What the hell!" I pull away to stare him down, my annoyance flaring. "You're never afraid to tell me how it is or how you think it should be, but for some reason, you have *no* opinion about our wedding? How is that possible?"

His jaw tenses. "Fine. You want to know what I think? I think we should get married now. *Today.* Or in three days, if that's when we can get a license. Hell, I was ready to sign those papers the day I put this on your finger." He reaches for my left hand, his thumb grazing my engagement ring. "Everyone who matters to me is already here, or will be, in a few hours. I don't want to spend the next year of my life stressing over some big party so a bunch of fucking people I've *never* talked to before and will probably never talk to again can tell me congratulations and hand me an envelope of cash. I don't want to listen to what other people want us to do. I don't want to get married in Toronto, or Oslo. I want to get married right *here,* right now. In Alaska, where I met you, where I fell in love with you, where I'm building a life with you."

He exhales deeply, as if relieved that he could finally pull the cork on that bottle and let it all out. When he speaks again, it's in a much slower, calmer tone. "But I get that I'm not the only one in this relationship and that weddings are a big deal for a lot of women, so if you want the big day and the big dress and the hundreds of people, then I'm okay with that, too."

"I don't." The moment I say it, I know it's true. I thought I did want all that, or that I might want it. But I'd much rather spend the next year living my life with Jonah than planning a single day.

Jonah's eyebrows arch. "You don't?"

"I mean, I want something nice and special. *Not* the community center, with recycled Christmas dinner decorations," I clarify. "And I want to wear a dress, but it doesn't have to be something I custom-ordered six months in advance. I want to be able to look back on our wedding day in fifty years from now as one of the best days of my life, but I don't need the big dog-and-pony show." I smile at Roy's words. "All I *need* is you. And the people who are around us right now."

Jonah's breath hitches. He reaches up to tuck a loose strand of hair beneath my knit cap. "So, what are you sayin', exactly?"

I struggle against the goofy grin that threatens to emerge as my excitement bubbles. "Roy did say I could pull a wedding out of my ass in a week and make it not suck."

Jonah frowns. "You talked to *Roy* about this?"

"I wanted an impartial opinion."

He barks with laughter. "Well, yeah, Roy definitely doesn't give a fuck about us getting married." He leans in to press his forehead against mine. "Then, we're doin' this? For real?"

I smile, even as nervous flutters stir in my stomach. "For real. If you're sure."

"We wouldn't be here if I wasn't." He lets out a slow, shaky breath. "Guess we should drive to Wasilla and get that marriage license, then."

"Yeah. After we drop off the eggs. And gravely disappoint my mother. And my best friend." A twinge of sadness pricks my chest. My mother won't be the only one disappointed; I'm about to devastate my best friend. "And I guess I'll call Muriel and tell her the good news?"

"She's still up at the house."

"*What?* You left her in there with them?"

"She said she was leaving, but she hasn't yet." Jonah's brow furrows. "They should be fine. Simon's there."

I groan and, collecting his hands, tug him toward the door.

CHAPTER EIGHT

I'm not sure what I expected to walk into, but Muriel, my mother, and Astrid sharing a laugh at the counter was certainly not it. The wedding magazines have been closed and stacked in a tidy pile, the broken coffee mug cleaned up as if it'd never happened.

Simon is still puttering at the stove.

And Björn is at the sink, quietly washing dishes.

"What the fuck happened while we were gone?" Jonah murmurs as we quietly shed our boots and outer things.

"Had to be Simon." He's always the voice of reason, though I don't know what he could have said to flip the mood so quickly. I hold up the carton. "Roy had a dozen."

"Oh! You're back. Brilliant. I think I've managed to keep everything else warm." Simon, still in his apron, trots over to collect the eggs, offering me a secretive wink. "It's your wedding. You tell us what you want and we'll happily fall in line."

"What about Mom-zilla over there?" I whisper.

He shushes me, but says, "Even her. Maybe not as happily, but she's already had two weddings of her own. If she wants a third, she'll have to divorce me first."

Muriel turns in her seat to offer her wide, face-transforming smile. "I was just tellin' them about the time Toby surprised a grizzly out behind the Ale House. He didn't have nothing on him and the thing wouldn't back off, no matter how much he yelled, so he did the only thing he could think of—broke out in a rendition of 'The Star-Spangled Banner.'" Muriel's shoulders shake with laughter.

"And what happened?" I ask curiously. Obviously nothing too horrific, because my friend is alive and well.

"Haven't you heard that boy try to carry a tune? The poor animal hightailed it outta there." Muriel is chuckling as she climbs off her stool. "I guess we should get this place set for brunch." She rounds the counter to the cupboard that holds our dishes. Sometimes I think she knows this kitchen better than I do. "Here, Björn. I could use your help. My right hip isn't what it used to be."

There's nothing wrong with Muriel's hip.

Before Björn realizes what's happening, she's handed him a stack of plates. "Go on. Over on that table Roy built for them. It's high time it got used."

With nothing more than a glance Jonah's way, he saunters over to set the table.

Astrid beckons Jonah with an outstretched hand. He closes the distance instantly. "I'm living the life I want to live, and I'm happy," she whispers, cupping his cheek. "Just as you are permitted to do."

He sighs heavily. "I'm sorry for being a jerk."

Mom catches my eye. Her brow pulls together as she mouths, "I'm sorry. I got carried away."

I smile and mouth back, "I know."

Mom rolls her eyes but then smiles. Her emotions sometimes lead her to act irrationally, especially when she has an idea in her head. At least she always sees it after the fact.

"What time are Agnes and Mabel arriving?" Muriel asks, her hands full of cutlery.

"They'll be here around one." I steal a glance Jonah's way to find him watching me closely, that crooked smile that is my downfall touching his lips. I reach for him and he sidles up beside me, curling his arm around my shoulder. I look to him—because he's truly the only one who matters here—when I add, "Which will give Jonah and me enough time to drive to the courthouse to apply for a marriage license, because we've decided we don't want to wait anymore."

There's a clatter of silverware, as Muriel empties her hands onto the table, freeing them to slap together in a loud clap. "Well, hot damn! We have ourselves a wedding to plan!" she exclaims, her voice full of uncharacteristic glee.

"Calla? You down there?" Jonah's deep voice booms from the top of the stairs.

"Yeah!"

"You callin' Diana?"

Shit. I need to do that, too. "Give me ten." I settle into my desk chair, the stack of identification and other paperwork that we need to apply for our license next to me.

Upstairs, I can hear the hum of voices. Astrid's reaction to our news was in line with Muriel's, though far more subdued. My mother, on the other hand, took a few deep breaths and then started talking out loud about an intimate wedding she arranged the flowers for a few years back and how lovely it turned out.

Now, they and Muriel are upstairs discussing the order of what needs to be booked, and what are our limited options. Obviously my mother will do the flowers and Astrid has graciously offered to bake the cake, but there are so many things up in the air.

I shake out my hands as I wait for my MacBook to power up. My frazzled nerves at the moment have nothing to do with the fact that Jonah and I are getting married next week, though. That decision, I'm confident in.

This one … not so much.

I open my email server and hit Compose.

Before I lose my nerve, I type out a message I pray will change someone's life as much as a phone call one night in July changed mine.

"If that's Jonah *again*, tell him we're five minutes from home." His worry is equal parts endearing and annoying.

My mom slides on her reading glasses to read the text. "It's Toby. He says that Muriel says Connie can do it—slow down, Calla. You're making me nervous."

I ease my foot on the brake pedal to navigate the right-hand turn onto our side road. When my mom, Agnes, Mabel, and I climbed into the Jeep at seven A.M., on a mission to Anchorage to find a wedding dress, the roads were clear and only the odd snowflake drifted from the sky. We had every intention of being back in time for a late lunch. But one failed bridal store led to the next, and then another, and by the time we hit the road for Trapper's Crossing, it was after one, and the winter storm the forecasters have been threatening us with was well on its way in.

"Connie who? I don't know any Connies."

"Well, *I* definitely don't know this Connie, but apparently she's sewn all the costumes for the school's drama club. Muriel's on her way over there now to ask her."

"And you told her the dress needs *major* alterations?" I had all but given up on finding *the* wedding dress after sifting through dozens of generic strapless ball gowns and over-the-top beaded options and was about to settle on a nice but "seen it a thousand times before" option when Agnes discovered a simple but elegant dress with a round neckline and long sleeves, buried deep within a rack. Even my mother approved. The only problem? It's several sizes too big. A problem that the bridal shop owner promised could easily be fixed with a skilled seamstress. Unfortunately, there is no way hers can get it done in time.

"Yes! Almost word for word." Mom reads her text message out loud to prove it.

"Okay. Well, if she thinks this Connie woman can do it, then I have to believe she can do it." I doubt there will be a lot of "asking" involved when poor Connie opens her door to a determined Muriel McGivney.

"You know, we're putting an awful lot of trust in your neighbor." Mom slides her reading glasses off. Her brow is pulled with worry. "I hope you're not disappointed in how this all turns out, Calla."

My stomach squeezes, that little voice in the back of my mind echoing her thoughts.

Once Jonah and I arrived home from the courthouse, it became a mad dash to get the ball rolling on making decisions. Simon suggested we call Muriel to help us. I agreed, and she arrived not twenty minutes later with an eight-and-a-half-by-eleven coil notebook tucked under her arm. Her bible, she called it—tattered and bent and marred with countless scribbled names and numbers—that would help us with the hows. But first we needed to decide on the when and where and who.

The when was easy. New Year's Eve. With the holidays, we won't get the license before the thirtieth and the parents are all leaving on January 2 so our window of opportunity is small.

As for the who, Jonah and I crafted a guest list on the drive to the courthouse. We came up with twenty-five people—more than I'd anticipated.

The where was the biggest challenge. There are only three wedding venues in the area and a few quick phone calls confirmed all were unavailable. Muriel was ready to pencil us into the community center despite my insistence that it lacked character and was too big for twenty-five people. We were resigned to cramming everyone into our house for a reception. And then Muriel was struck with an epiphany—the Ale House. It's cozy, it has character, and with a bit of elbow grease, she was convinced it could be ideal.

Best of all, it's close and available.

I had to admit, it wasn't the worst idea, and it would keep the chaos out of our house, which is already chaotic enough with all the guests.

Mom cautiously suggested we see "this Ale House of yours" before we committed to a wedding reception there.

So we drove over, and Mom spent a half hour walking in circles, pointing at things that would need to be put away or cleaned up—the cluttered bulletin board, the cheap folding tables, the fishing trophies.

Muriel agreed without argument. Shockingly.

My mother's exact words were, "I can work with this."

And so it was decided that our reception would take place at the Ale House.

With the biggest decisions nailed down, Muriel began listing all our resource options, both obvious and unconventional, given the tight timeline. Twenty-one-year-old Lacey Burns, who won a photography competition for her candid high school yearbook pictures and happens to be home from college for Christmas break; Michael and Anne Bowering, music teachers who play seven instruments and sing at church every Sunday; Gloria from the Winter Carnival planning community, who has been taking culinary classes in Anchorage for years, and is the best cook Muriel knows.

There wasn't a question she couldn't answer or a quandary she couldn't recommend a solution for.

Muriel was in her element.

And I've never valued her more.

A few hours and a dozen phone calls later, we had a photographer, musicians, and our caterer lined up. My mother phoned every florist between Wasilla and Anchorage to survey our options for flowers, and Astrid was throwing cake flavors at me.

It all seems too easy.

Maybe it is. Maybe this is going to be a disaster.

"She's marrying Jonah. It's going to be perfect, no matter what happens," Agnes, always the angel on my shoulder, chirps from the back seat.

Mom seems to absorb that. She turns to meet Agnes's gaze. "You know what? You're right. Calla is marrying her sky cowboy—"

"Oh God, Mom!" I cringe through the chorus of laughter.

But she's right.

I'm marrying Jonah.

In eight days, I'll be Mrs. Calla Riggs.

The wife of the furry-faced dickhead pilot who all but wrote me off that day Agnes sent him to pick me up from the airport. Who would've ever seen this coming? Certainly not me.

Butterflies erupt in my stomach as my attention drifts to the diamond snowflake on my finger. Jonah had a custom band made at the same time, but he has refused to show it to me, and I have yet to unearth his hiding place. Not for lack of trying.

Suddenly it dawns on me. "I need a ring for him!" I completely forgot.

"*Oh*. Right." My mom's deep frown says she forgot, too.

I check the clock. It's after three P.M. on Christmas Eve. "I'll drop you guys off and see if I can find something in Wasilla."

"What? No. You're not going back out today. This storm is getting worse by the minute." My mom shakes her head firmly.

"But he *needs* a ring." Guilt stirs inside me that this is the first I've thought of it. Jonah's always been so considerate, with the plane pendant that he flew hours away to have custom made, and with my engagement ring.

"We can find one on Thursday," Agnes promises. "Men's wedding bands are simple. He won't want anything flashy."

"Yeah, but they'll have to resize it. He's got those big yeti hands."

Mabel, whose enthusiasm over dress shopping dwindled half an hour into the first store and who's mainly sulked for the remainder of the time, snorts.

"Will he even wear it? I mean, he doesn't seem the jewelry type. You know, your father would leave his band lying around the house *all the time*. I'd get so mad at him. He finally lost it once and for all while out flying one day."

"Jonah needs one for the day. It doesn't matter if he wears it later." Though he had better.

"We got your dress today. We'll get the ring on Thursday. No problem. It'll all work out."

I steal a glance in my rearview mirror to meet Agnes's crinkled eyes. "I need a pair of your rose-colored glasses."

Her smile widens. "That's convenient because I got you a pair for Christmas."

My phone rings over the Bluetooth system then and a second later, Diana's name appears on my Jeep's screen.

"We'll be home in five minutes. You can talk to her then." My mom wrings her hands nervously.

When I called Diana yesterday to explain the situation, she shrieked, told me she hated me, and then demanded that I not replace her with some imposter until I've heard back from her. I've been anxiously awaiting her call ever since.

I hit the answer button on my steering wheel. "Tell me you have good news?" I hold my breath.

"Get that hot tub ready because your maid of honor is arriving next Monday night!" Diana's voice blasts over the Jeep's speakers.

"Seriously? You made it work? Oh my God!" I shriek, a thrill coursing through me.

"Alaska, twice in one year! This is *crazy*!"

Tears sting my eyes and the weight on my chest lifts. "You have no idea how happy I am! I *hated* the idea of getting married without you here!"

"Calla, slow down!" my mom yells over our excited chatter.

I feel the moment my tires lose traction as we're rounding the bend. On instinct, my foot slams on my brake, sending us careening off the road.

CHAPTER NINE

"What do you mean you're *not* calling him?" My mother is brushing caked snow off her jeans when she pauses to glare at me. "What *else* are we supposed to do?" She throws a hand at the front end of my Jeep, barely poking out from the ditch, its grill facing the sky.

"Call a tow truck?" It comes out as a question; it isn't much of one.

There was a moment of sheer terror as I gripped the useless steering wheel and we slid down the steep embankment; I was bracing myself for a flip or a crash into the tree line. Thankfully, we spun just enough to slide in backward and my Jeep landed in the snow with a thud and a crunch, leaving us with nothing more than racing hearts. After a nervous chorus of "Is everyone okay? I'm okay. Are you all okay?" and reassuring a panicked Diana, who listened in horror to the entire ordeal, we tested our doors.

Escaping the vehicle was a challenge. Climbing out of the gully in knee-deep snow was an *almost* comical level of hell—one that has left my mother in a sour mood over her ruined suede ankle boots.

"If you had just *listened* to me—"

"*Stop*." I hold up a hand. "Give me a minute to think, okay?" I feel like an idiot. I *was* going too fast around that bend given the snow cover. I *was* distracted. And I made a rookie mistake, hitting the brakes the way I did.

And I am *never* going to hear the end of this from Jonah.

Mom takes a deep, calming breath. "You know what? No one's hurt. We're only a couple miles from home. It's Christmas Eve. We're going to laugh about this later." She sounds like she's trying to convince herself.

I leave her to it. "How bad is it?" I call out to Agnes, who's trudging around in the ditch, her short legs disappearing with each step as she surveys the situation.

"We won't know until we pull it out of here, but we're definitely not gonna be able to drive it out. Does Jonah have a winch?"

"I don't know. Maybe. What's a winch?" Phil left so many tools in the workshop.

"I doubt it'd be strong enough on that old truck of yours, anyway." She looks much like a child, packed in that oversized parka and using her mitt-covered hands to climb out to the road on all fours.

"Kelly's coming to get me," Mabel announces. Her thumbs fly over her phone's screen, sending a response to her new best friend, a fourteen-year-old girl she met at the farmers' market this past summer. "Her house is, like, two minutes from here."

Agnes's brow furrows. "Don't you want to spend time with—"

"I'll be back for dinner."

After a moment, Agnes simply nods. She may be frustrated with her daughter, but she'll never outright scold her. That's never been Agnes's way. It also could end up being her downfall, raising a headstrong teenaged girl on her own.

Agnes shifts her attention back to me, blinking against the flurry of snowflakes that even her deep cowl can't shield. "Do the McGivneys have a winch?"

"Maybe, but I feel like I'm asking them for help for *everything* lately. I don't want to drag Toby out on Christmas Eve, into *this*." It seems to be getting worse, the wind picking up to the point that the only relief from snowflakes in my eyes is looking down at the ground. I groan. "I'm sorry. This was my fault."

"We'll figure it out." She pats my arm. "But we might as well get back to your place. It's getting dark, and I'm guessing it'll be awhile before any truck makes their way out here."

"I guess I can't avoid him anymore, can I?"

Agnes offers a sympathetic smile. "He can be a pain in the butt, but it's only because he cares about you *so much*."

With a resigned sigh, I reach into my pocket for my phone.

"Hello, Simon?" My mom's voice carries. "I need you to come get us. We're down the road. Calla put her Jeep in the ditch ..."

"*Ugh*. Great." Jonah's going to be pissed that he didn't hear about this from me. This keeps getting worse!

Agnes nods toward something in the distance. "Someone's coming."

I follow her line of sight to the set of headlights. It can't be Kelly, who will be riding a snowmachine. Jonah and Simon are at home with our only other vehicles.

There's only one person who lives beyond us on this road, and he doesn't get any visitors.

We edge to the side as the big black truck crawls forward, coming to a stop beside us.

"Do you know him?" my mom asks.

"That's Roy."

"*The* Roy?" My mom gives me a look.

"Whatever he says, don't take it personally," I warn her, though I told him long ago that I might put up with his bullshit, but if he tried it on my loved ones, he'd be dead to me.

"*That* is a winch," Agnes says over the rumbling engine, nodding at the front grill where something that looks like a spool of wire is mounted.

"And *that's* a grinch," I counter quietly, earning Mabel's giggle.

The driver's side opens with a creak and Roy hops out, tugging that Davy Crockett raccoon-fur hat Jonah loathes so much onto his head. He rounds the front of his truck. His weathered face looks none too pleased as he inspects my predicament.

I decide on humor to kick things off. "My first foray into off-roading didn't go as planned."

The corner of his mouth kicks up a notch. "I see that."

Agnes offers him that wide smile. "Hello again, Roy. I don't know if you remember us. I'm Agnes. That's my daughter, Mabel. We met in August."

He makes a grunting sound that could be considered an acknowledgment, but then adds, "The night Calla shot that bear."

Agnes nods. "That was quite the night."

I gesture toward my mother. "Roy, this is my mom, Susan."

"Roy." She forgoes offering a handshake—her arms wrapped tightly around her body for warmth—and dips her head in greeting. "Calla has told me so much about you. She took me to see the cabin. Your work is impeccable."

He studies her a moment before nodding once, and then he turns back to my Jeep. "Everyone all right?"

"Yeah, we're fine. Just a little shaken up. Could have been worse, though, right?"

"You goin' too fast, like usual?"

"*See*? I told you! I *told* her," my mom exclaims triumphantly.

"And then she hit the brakes. You *never* hit the brakes like that when you're sliding," Mabel adds matter-of-factly.

Roy frowns at her. "How old are you again?"

Mabel adjusts her stance as if she's trying to make herself appear taller. "Thirteen and a half." Though she could pass for sixteen, with her sleek chin-length bob and angular jawline.

"Sounds like you're already a better driver than Calla."

Oh my God. "Okay, are we done here?" I snap.

Roy smirks. "Jonah on his way?"

"Yeah, that's a safe bet." And I'm sure he'll be here momentarily.

Roy eyes my Jeep, then his truck, then the winch, and then finally his gaze lands on my mother, who chose to wear her lighter shopping jacket instead of her parka and is shuddering uncontrollably. "You should go on and sit in my truck where it's warm."

She rushes for the passenger side, uttering a breezy thank-you.

"You, too, if you want," he adds to Mabel.

"Nah, I'm good. My friend's on her way here to get me. I think that's her." She points to a small approaching light in the distance.

Roy slips on his gloves and, stooping in front of his truck, unfastens a heavy-duty orange hook. "What were you guys doin' out in this, anyway?" If I didn't know better, there's a touch of scolding in his tone.

"Shopping."

"Actually, we were out looking for a wedding dress for Calla. Did you hear the good news yet?" As usual, Agnes speaks to him as if he cares. "They're getting married on New Year's Eve!"

He merely grunts in response.

Kelly coasts in then on her dad's yellow-and-black snow-machine.

"Excuse me." Agnes leaves us to walk over and talk to Mabel before she takes off.

I perk my ears to try to catch the conversation over the idling engine. I'm sure I hear Agnes say five o'clock. I'm also sure that Mabel will come back later than that. More and more, she seems to be testing her mother's patience, which is endless with Agnes —a flaw in this regard. Jonah and I have already discussed the need to step in and keep Mabel in line when they move here next summer. How Mabel will respond to that, I can't guess.

"You find one?" Roy's grating voice cuts into my thoughts.

"Huh?"

"A dress."

"Oh. Yeah. But I have to get it basically cut in half to fit me. Hopefully it still looks like a dress after it's dissected."

"I'm sure it'll look fine." He yanks on the cord to unfurl the wire.

And I quietly watch him.

Does he ever wonder what Delyla looked like on her wedding day? Does he regret not being there to walk her down the aisle? Does it burn deep, knowing that his replacement, this man who Nicole spent thirty happy years with, likely did?

How often does Roy think about his daughter, especially now that she's no longer just a distant memory, a cherub-cheeked toddler in a thirty-odd-year-old department store portrait?

Now that he knows she has thought about him, at least enough to sit down and write that letter?

These are all questions I wish I could ask. If Roy were anyone else, I would.

"So, I guess you decided to pull a weddin' out of your ass, then?"

"I did. We're having a reception at the Ale House for family and close friends. Muriel promised to take all the dead animals and tacky signs down and my mom is a florist, so she can make pretty much *anything* look nice."

With mention of my mom, Roy steals a glance into his truck's cab, where she sits huddled. "You look like her."

I smile. "Yeah, I've heard that once or twice."

His jaw works as if he's going to say something else, but he must decide against it, choosing silence instead.

"So, you're going to come, right?"

"To what? Your wedding? Why on *earth* would you want *me* there?"

I was expecting some lame excuse, but his response catches me off guard. Or rather, it's the genuine shock in his voice that surprises me. "Because I do?" I can't come up with a better response at the moment. His name is on our guest list, below our family, but ahead of Marie, and George and Bobbie. He's in that in-between category, along with Agnes, Mabel, and the McGivneys—people who may not be in the blood-related "family" bucket but don't fit into the "friends" bucket. They're those important people who are woven into the fabric of our daily lives, and their absence would surely leave holes should they disappear.

It's a long time before he answers. "I got nothin' to wear to a wedding."

There's the lame excuse. "I'm sure you could figure something out. Does that mean you'll come?"

He peers down the road behind me. "That must be help."

He didn't answer my question, I note.

The headlights are coming from the direction of our house and they're closing in fast. I know even before I spot the bearded driver that it's Jonah behind the wheel of the BMW. Simon isn't in the passenger seat.

He executes a perfect three-point turn in the snow with speed I wouldn't hazard even on a sunny summer day. He then hops out and marches toward us with his boots unfastened and his coat unzipped, as if he dressed while running out the door. "What happened?" He has that urgent, almost menacing tone that he gets when he's panicked.

"I slid into the ditch."

"No shit. Are you okay?"

"We're fine." I heard my mom tell Simon as much, but of course Jonah needed to witness that with his own two eyes. He's always been a "see it to believe it" kind of person.

He shakes his head. "I *told* you the roads were getting bad. You should've come back *hours* ago—"

"I found a dress!" I exclaim, trying to distract him from his rant.

His shoulders lift with a deep inhale. A telltale sign that he's fighting his need to continue rebuking me. "It's what you wanted?"

"It's perfect. Or it will be."

He exhales. "Good. I'm glad."

My mom slides out of Roy's truck, slamming the heavy door shut behind her. "Simon didn't come with you?"

"I told him to hang back. Why don't you guys take the car and head home? I'll help Roy get this out."

Mom slows to smile at Roy but only for long enough to say, "Thank you for your help. I hope we see you again soon," before rushing ahead to climb into the driver's side.

"Don't they get snow in Toronto?" Roy asks casually, inspecting the underside of my Jeep. I'm guessing he's looking for somewhere to attach that big hook.

"Yes. And she hates it there, too."

Jonah notices Mabel strapping on a spare helmet. "Where's she goin'?"

"Out with Kelly for a while."

He frowns. "It's *Christmas Eve*."

"I know, but Agnes told her—"

"Mabel!" he barks. "I want to see you back at our house by four thirty!"

Even in the dusk, I can see her face twist with indignation. "But Mom said—"

"I'll be watching the clock. And Kelly? You go slow on that. It's a lot faster than it needs to be." A warning he makes every time Mabel and Kelly have gone out sledding together.

Mabel turns away, but not before I catch the eye roll.

Jonah doesn't miss it, either, based on his inward groan.

"You're gonna make her hate you."

"That's fine. At least she'll live." He zips up his coat. "Go on, get out of here. It's miserable out."

Jonah's being far more tolerable than I expected. "You're going to give me another earful later, aren't you?"

"Yup." He leans in to kiss me. "But it's only because I love you. See you at home."

I smile sheepishly. "Thank you."

"Oh, you'll be thanking me later." He slaps my backside on his way past.

"Hey, Roy. Christmas dinner at our place tomorrow night. Come around four?"

He spares me a glance before turning back to my Jeep to fasten the hook. "Got plans already."

I sigh heavily. "Right. Christmas with the chickens."

"And the goats," he hollers after me.

I fight against heavy eyelids as I burrow beneath our duvet, sated with food and wine, waiting for Jonah to come to bed. He and Roy battled the blizzard for close to an hour, working to haul my Jeep out of the ditch. I spent that time tackling the endless pile of dishes Astrid dirtied while cooking until my guilt over my carelessness overwhelmed me.

I was yanking on my boots, ready to take the snowmachine out to check on them, when the approaching glow of my Jeep's headlights appeared in our driveway.

Surprisingly, it sustained minimal damage in the crash—shattered brake lights, a few scratches along the bumper, and a dent that Jonah says is cosmetic. All things that are easily fixed.

Jonah was too tired and cold to give me any grief, and thankfully my mother laid off on the blame game, too busy settled into the chair by the fire with Astrid's mulled wine and my laptop, researching rustic winter reception décor ideas for the Ale House.

What started out as a hectic day transformed into an enjoyable night of food, family, and laughter. Astrid presented plate after plate of hearty Norwegian dishes—pork ribs she called *ribbe,* tender boiled potatoes, brussels sprouts and red cabbage from our garden haul, and a gelatinous cod dish called lutefisk that I swiftly passed on. After dinner, Jonah tore off the roof of the gingerbread house and then parked himself on the couch to watch Christmas movies, while Björn busted out the Swords and Shields board game. Even Mabel was interested in learning how to play, and I was hit with a wave of nostalgia as I watched her frown of consternation and listened to her competitive trash talk. For a few hours tonight, we had the old Mabel back—the one who used to sit across from my father at his checkerboard night after night.

"Come on, Jonah," I groan. If this were any other time, I'd holler for him to get his ass up here. But everyone else said their good-nights well over an hour ago and the house is silent, save for Björn's steady snore.

I reach for my phone to send Diana a Merry Christmas text that she'll get when she wakes up.

My heart skips a beat when I see the notification.

Delyla answered the email I sent her yesterday morning.

My thumbs fumble to open the message. I hold my breath as I read the lengthy response.

I'm on my second reread when Jonah strolls into our bedroom, peeling his sweater over his head as he shuts our door. "I won't be surprised if the power gets knocked out all day tomorrow. At least the generators are ready to go ..." His voice drifts. "What's wrong?"

I let out a shaky breath. "Roy's daughter wrote me back."

His eyes bulge. "You actually contacted her?"

"Yesterday." With all the wedding frenzy, I didn't have time to mention it. To be honest, a part of me didn't want to mention it, not until I knew if my efforts were worthwhile. If Delyla would even respond to the woman who lives down the road from her estranged father.

She responded all right.

Jonah tosses his sweater onto the dresser. "*And?*"

"And she thanked me for contacting her. She wants me to call her." Whenever I'm free, the sooner the better. There was no missing the impatience and enthusiasm in her words.

He sheds the rest of his clothes, changing into a thermal flannel sleep set I bought him. "Are you going to?"

"Call her? Of course. This is Roy's second chance."

"What if he doesn't want a second chance?"

"He does. I *know* he does. He wouldn't have kept the card and those pictures if he didn't."

"And when she asks why you're the one calling, and not her father?"

"I'll tell her the truth. That I think he's scared."

Jonah seems to consider that as he yanks off his wool socks and tosses them into the hamper in the corner. "You're doing something good for him, even if he won't see it like that."

"You know what? Even if he hates me for a while, if it means he could have a relationship with his daughter, it'll be worth it." I wonder if Agnes felt this same nervousness when she went behind my father's back to call me.

With a sigh that rings of exhaustion, Jonah peels off his watch and sets it onto the nightstand before lifting the duvet to slide in.

He freezes, his eyebrows popping, and it's then I remember the scandalous red lace and white faux-fur-trimmed baby doll dress I slipped on tonight, partially hidden beneath my pajama top while I waited. I bought it two weeks ago while shopping in Anchorage. An impulse purchase, sparked when I walked past a department store's Christmas lingerie section and decided maybe Jonah would like me in something other than oversized flannel.

"Merry early Christmas," I say coyly. I was eager to show him this an hour ago. Now, my limbs have been lulled by a soft mattress, my skin accustomed to the warmth. I reach for the covers to tug them closer.

He's too fast, though, yanking them down and making me shudder. "I need you to get up and walk around for me a bit."

"It's cold!" I whine, though watching the heat ignite in his stare stirs desire in my lower belly.

"Speaking of cold, do you want to hear about how I froze my balls off, sitting in a ditch for an hour during a blizzard on Christmas Eve because my soon-to-be wife has a lead foot?"

My heart leaps with that title, even as he criticizes my driving. "Fine." I slip from the comfort of our bed, smoothing my hands over my hips as my bare feet touch the cool wood floor. I let the unbuttoned flannel top slide off my arms and tumble off, earning his curse.

The bed creaks under Jonah's hefty weight as he settles in, shucking the shirt he just pulled on to reveal that ribbed torso and muscular chest I've spent countless hours splayed across.

"Any special requests?"

Linking his fingers together behind his head, he lies back against his pillow and bites his lip in thought. "What's underneath that?"

"Not much," I tease, my pulse racing. Even now, I still catch hints of that same nervousness I felt the night we were stranded in the safety cabin and stripping off our rain-soaked clothes in front of each other.

"Turn around." His voice has taken on that gravelly sound I love.

I oblige, making a slow circle to the sound of Jonah's sharp inhale.

"Show me."

My fingertips are grazing the faux fur-trimmed hem when the power cuts, throwing us into pitch-black darkness.

"Are you *fucking* kidding me!" Jonah's roar of frustration carries into the night.

CHAPTER TEN

I wake to Jonah's soft lips on mine and his beard tickling my skin. "Merry Christmas," he whispers, his voice husky with sleep.

"Merry Christmas." I revel in his warmth for a long moment, lingering in that comfortable space where I could close my eyes and drift away. But a murky predawn sky pokes in from the gap in the poorly drawn curtain, suggesting we've slept much later than usual. "What time is it?"

"After nine. The power's still out."

I groan. I can't say when we actually fell asleep, but it was late, after what felt like hours of slow, torturous play in the dark, the challenge of keeping silent in the still night while making the other break a game we were both eager to win.

"I need to get moving, but I didn't want you to wake up without me."

I smile. "That's sweet."

He kisses me again. "Yeah. That's me. Sweet."

"Is that what you called what you did to me last night?" I wouldn't be surprised if I have a map of fingerprint bruises marring my flesh.

His chuckle vibrates deep in my chest as he slips out of the bed, stark naked and unbothered by the chill in the air. He peels back the curtain to peek outside, revealing a thick frame of snow along the sill.

"Is there a lot?" I murmur, distracted by his sculpted muscles and his morning erection as I burrow deeper into the covers.

"I'd say almost two feet fell overnight."

"*Wow.*"

"Yeah. Might be even worse than last year's storm." He squints as he peers up at the sky. "At least it's slowed down a bit. It'll make plowing the driveway easier."

"Seriously? On Christmas? You're a workhorse." Though sometimes I think that tractor is more a toy to Jonah than anything labor-related.

"Well, *yeah*. Muriel and them will want to drive up for dinner."

"Yeah. I guess." I add, "And Roy."

He snorts. "Babe, Roy's not comin' to Christmas dinner."

"We'll see." He's likely right, but I refuse to give up on the curmudgeon just yet.

I admire Jonah's body as he tugs on his thermal clothes, followed by his outer clothes. "I'll be down in a bit," I promise.

He's at the door when he stoops to retrieve my slinky outfit from its heap in the corner. He holds it up by his pinkie. "I'm getting a repeat performance tonight, right?"

I plaster mock sympathy across my face. "Oh, I'm so sorry, but Mrs. Claus only comes out on Christmas Eve."

His responding smile is wicked. "We'll see about that."

I emerge twenty minutes later to Michael Bublé's "White Christmas" playing over a portable speaker, competing with the hum of the generator outside. Björn is stuffing a log into an already blazing fire in the hearth while Astrid sits on the couch, studying the designs for the log house we're breaking ground on in the spring. Balsam fir–scented candles burn in place of table lamps.

Meanwhile in the kitchen, Simon is wrist-deep in the raw turkey, the aroma of onions and sausage lingering in the air. My mother watches, her customary mimosa perched artfully in her grasp.

"Merry Christmas!" I raise my eyebrows at Simon. "You aren't wasting time."

"It's a twenty-five-pound bird! It's going to take a few hours." Simon nods to our oven. "It's a good thing you went with propane, or we might be eating cold leftovers."

"Pretty sure we could survive all winter out here, if we had to." Between the Toyostove and a winter's worth of wood for the fireplace, we'll always have heat. For our electrical needs, we have a heavy-duty generator, as well as a backup generator and enough fuel sitting in the workshop to keep them running for months. "But I need to put the breakfast casserole in there for an hour before you put the turkey in."

"Already in and baking. The note said 350°?" Mom rounds the counter and ropes her arms around me, pulling me into a fierce hug. "Merry Christmas, honey. We're *so happy* to be spending it with you guys. Here, I poured you one." She holds up the second champagne flute for me, but then pulls her hand back. "That is assuming you *can* drink alcohol." She levels me with an examining stare.

She's *still* not convinced that this isn't a shotgun wedding. "Oh my God, Mom! How many mulled wines did I have last night?" I snatch the glass from her hand and punctuate that with a large gulp.

The side door cracks open. "Ho ho ho!" comes Agnes's reedy voice, along with boot stomps outside the threshold. She appears down the hall, rosy-cheeked from the cold and stooping under the weight of a cranberry-colored canvas satchel half her size slung over her shoulder. A green-and-gold-wrapped box pokes out from the open end.

Astrid sets the blueprints on the coffee table to rise and help her. "You didn't ride across the lake with that, did you?"

"No, no. Jonah brought it over in the truck last night." She sheds her parka and her hat to reveal a tacky red reindeer Christmas sweater. "Boy, there's a lot of snow out there."

"And more coming later, according to the forecast." Astrid lugs the heavy bag over to the Christmas tree, where people have been covertly tucking packages over the last few days. Luggage restrictions didn't seem to limit anyone. A sizeable and colorful stack of presents now covers most of the tree skirt.

Agnes rubs her hands together for warmth, stopping at the kitchen counter. "Can I help you with something, Simon?"

"Yes! You can help me by pouring yourself a mimosa or a coffee and putting your feet up for the day. We're *all* covered." He caps that off with a beguiling smile.

"Sounds like my kind of Christmas."

I set the mimosa down to fix myself a latte. "Is Mabel still sleeping?"

Agnes chuckles. "No. This is the one day of the year that I *don't* have to drag her out of bed. She went to feed Bandit and Zeke for Jonah. He said he has to go to the hangar for something."

I drop my spoon with a clatter. "He's going to the hangar?"

"Yes."

"*Now?*"

"Yes." She frowns. "Why?"

As if on cue, the snowmachine's engine starts.

I abandon my coffee with a huff and rush for the door. "Because his Christmas present is out there, and he wasn't supposed to find it yet!"

Jonah's back is to me when I push through the door a few minutes later, my scarf haphazardly wrapped around my neck, my cheeks raw from the futile race to get here ahead of him.

In front of him is the satin steel-gray Chevy Silverado that Toby drove over last night.

"Guess I should have asked about getting a winch for it?"

He looks over his shoulder and gives me an arched brow before he turns back to stare at it some more. "What did you do now, Barbie?"

I assume that's a rhetorical question. "I noticed you eying Steve's truck when they were here." The contractor who restored the old cabin couldn't stop raving about his. I shimmy up behind Jonah and wrap my arms around his waist. "And I knew you'd never buy one for yourself."

"That's because it's a fucking expensive truck."

"So was my Jeep."

"Yeah, but …" His voice drifts, his eyes drifting to the old Beaver, sitting in pieces. I know what he's thinking—he's spending a lot of money on a plane he doesn't really need, but he's doing it in a bid to honor my father.

"But *nothing*. Phil's old truck is unreliable, and you need a vehicle of your own. One that doesn't fly. You can keep this for the next twenty-five years if you want."

"They don't make trucks to last that long anymore." With a groan, he turns and collects me in his arms. "This is *way too* much. But thank you."

"I disagree. And you're welcome." I stretch onto my tiptoes and let my lips linger on his in a tender kiss. "I can't believe you didn't guess. I dropped enough hints."

"That you're crazy? Yeah, I knew that."

I pinch his side. "Did you check out the inside yet?"

"Honestly, I'm afraid to."

I laugh and grab his hands, tugging him toward the driver's side. The key is sitting in the console where Toby said he left it. "It was so much fun, picking everything out." I hit the ignition button and the truck roars to life. The sound of church bells and children's voices singing a Christmas carol blasts over the radio. "And look how much room there is in here!"

Jonah peers around the cab. "Björn won't have much to complain about on his ride back to the airport. Lemme in."

I clamber over the console to the passenger seat.

He climbs in, shutting the door behind him. Finally, I see the glimmer of delight in his eyes. "This is nice, Calla." He steps on the gas pedal and revs the engine. "*Really* nice."

"I know. I almost gave it to you early, because I couldn't wait any longer." I peel off my gloves and hit buttons to get the heat going. The initial gust of cold air blows through the vents, but it'll grow warm in a few minutes.

His hands smooth over the steering wheel. He pauses in thought. "I guess I should give you your present now, then?"

"It's *here*?" I peer out the window to search the hangar. Jonah's been tight-lipped. I have no idea what's in store for me, but I'm bracing myself for at least one gag gift.

"It's right *here*." He reaches into his coat pocket and pulls out a small, letter-sized envelope. With a crooked smile, he hands it to me.

I tear open the seal and fish out the papers. And squeal. "Are you serious?"

He chuckles. "It was supposed to be just a winter getaway, but I guess it'll be a honeymoon now."

I scan through the details of the seven-day, all-inclusive trip to Hawaii for two in mid-January. I've been bugging him for months to fly somewhere warm this winter, but he never seemed keen on the idea of a resort, claiming he'd be bored, lying around a beach all day. As usual though, he's been scheming behind my back.

"Oh my God, this is *amazing*! Thank you!" I throw myself at him, seizing his face and dropping hard, feverish kiss after kiss against his lips.

I finally relent, only to be pulled back, his hand firmly gripping my nape. The kiss he treats me to is not feverish or quick, but long and slow and deep, his tongue coaxing my lips apart.

My hands wander of their own accord, over that sexy, sharp jut of his throat, over the ridges of his broad chest, along his powerful thighs and up, in between, to where he has grown hard. Warmth instantly floods my core, the anticipation of his touch making my pulse soar. I stretch my body across the console in my bid to get closer to him.

"That's a big extended cab back there," he murmurs against my mouth.

I feel the insinuation deep inside. "You should probably test it out." My voice is breathless as I blindly paw at the truck's dash, searching for the heat controls.

He inhales sharply, his intense gaze boring into mine. "Good idea. *We* should."

I shed my coat, kick off my boots, and scramble to the back seat. By the time Jonah has shucked his coat, exited the driver's side, and is opening the back passenger-side door to climb in, I've already shed my outer clothes and got my pajama pants tugged down to my ankles, my bare skin impervious to the cold.

"I seem to recall having one in this shade a few years ago." Simon holds up the robin's egg sweater vest for all to see. "It mysteriously disappeared."

There was nothing "mysterious" about it. My mother takes it upon herself to purge his wardrobe of anything she deems "ratty." I used to think she was overstepping when it came to managing her husband's attire, but half of Jonah's closet consists of things

I've ordered, and I'm constantly filtering through his drawers, tossing threadbare socks and shirts.

"And now you have a new one!" my mom exclaims, inhaling her bottle of perfume and humming with delight, as if it's the first time she's ever smelled it. Simon buys her a new one every year. That's what their gift exchange consists of—sweater vests and a year's supply of perfume.

I smile as I wonder what Jonah and I will be exchanging on Christmas morning ten, fifteen, twenty years from now. Likely not vacations and bodily fluids in the back of a brand-new pickup truck.

Astrid stoops to search beneath the tree. "All that's left are gifts for Muriel and the men. I think that's it."

"In our household, we had a two-gift limit." Björn eyeballs the mountain of strewn paper and ribbons littering the floor. I heard him mutter the same Norwegian word several times as he sat back and watched parcel after parcel change hands for nearly two hours. My guess is it wasn't anything positive.

"It's not your household, though, is it?" Jonah murmurs before devouring a shortbread cookie.

"Thank you, everyone!" Mabel is all smiles as she sets her pile —mainly clothes and gift cards—on the floor beside the couch. With that tucked away, she climbs from her seat and bolts for the coat rack, her phone in hand.

Jonah frowns after her. "Where're you going? Where's she going?"

"Out for a ride with Kelly, while it's not snowing."

Jonah opens his mouth—to complain that it's Christmas and Mabel's place is here, no doubt.

I stuff the shortbread cookie I was about to eat into his mouth. "Leave her alone," I whisper, giving his knee a squeeze. "Plus, she has a small gift for Kelly that she wants to give her."

He chews the cookie while he thinks. "Take the blue one. It has more gas."

She smiles.

"And be back in an hour."

"Okay, Jonah," she says, drawing out his name. At least she doesn't seem irritated.

"Oh, what's that in there? I think we missed something." Agnes sticks her hand into the branches of the tree to retrieve a small box that I suspect she put there. She holds it out to pretend to read the label—there's no label from what I can see—before trekking over to hand it to Jonah. "This one's for you."

Jonah looks curiously at it, then at me—I shrug, because I have no clue—and then at her. "What is it?"

She shrugs. "Open it and find out."

He picks at the corner of the tape until he manages to catch it. In seconds, he has unraveled the paper and is opening the small jewelry box. Inside is a simple white gold ring.

Jonah nudges my side with his elbow. "Is this from you?"

I shake my head, studying the brushed finish and flat edge. "No, but it's *really* nice." And timely, given less than twenty-four hours ago, I was panicking over having forgotten that he needed one. How on earth did Agnes manage this?

"You bought me my wedding band, Aggie? Is this a proposal?" There's humor in his voice.

"Not exactly." Agnes and my mom exchange a nervous look. "I found that ring when I was clearing out Wren's house in the spring. It had somehow wedged itself between the baseboard and the carpet in his bedroom. I figured it might have been his, but I took a picture and sent it to Susan."

"It's the one I bought him. I remember picking it out, thinking it was simple but not boring. All the men's rings I'd looked at were *so* boring." My mom's voice has grown husky as she chuckles, her eyes glossy. "He was always taking it off while he was touching engines and other dirty things at work. I guess that's why he was so sure he'd lost it while out flying, but it must have fallen out of his pocket at home."

"It was lost in that house for twenty-five *years?*"

"Somewhere around there." Mom absently reaches for Simon's hand, weaving her fingers through his. "When Agnes asked what I thought about passing it on to Jonah, I honestly wasn't sure. I thought maybe you'd think it was bad luck or something—"

"No." Jonah's head shake is fervent, his brow furrowed as he studies it intently. "I don't think that at all."

Mom sighs as if a weight has been lifted off her shoulders. She smiles. "Agnes said you'd say something like that."

"This is … thank you." His Adam's apple bobs with a hard swallow.

I find myself doing the same, my own emotions stirring, though I can't be certain why—is it that Jonah will be wearing my father's wedding ring, or that my father, who I grew to love fiercely, meant so much to the man I'm about to marry?

"We'll have to have it resized after the wedding," I warn him. Wren Fletcher wasn't a small man, but Jonah overshadowed him.

"No, you won't." Agnes grins. "I already had it done."

Jonah slides the band onto his left ring finger. It fits perfectly. "How did you know—"

"When you were in the hospital, after the plane crash. You were all drugged up and sleeping. I tied a string to your finger and brought that to the jeweler. It worked!"

In one sudden, smooth motion, he stands and lifts Agnes off the ground and into a bear hug, spinning her tiny body around once before putting her back down. "What would we ever do without you, Aggie?"

She chuckles as she adjusts her Christmas sweater and then turns to me. "See, Calla? We told you it would all work out."

"Now you don't have to feel guilty about forgetting Jonah's ring," my mom adds.

Jonah's mouth falls open, in that dramatic way that tells me he's about to be a royal pain in my ass.

I groan. "Thanks, Mom."

"You *forgot* that I needed a ring?"

Here we go. I climb off the couch and start collecting wrapping paper. "It's not easy planning a wedding in a week. Over Christmas. In Alaska."

Jonah plucks the trash bag from his mother and trails behind me. He's still wearing the wedding band. "You didn't forget your dress."

"Well, no! It's my *wedding dress*."

"And the matching shoes?"

"There was a shoe store next door." He obviously saw the box in the back of the Jeep.

"Do you even need me at the wedding, or will I be in the way?"

"You're being ridiculous." I laugh and toss a ball of paper at his face.

Knuckles rap on the glass to the side entrance a second before a deep male voice hollers, "Ho! Ho! Ho!" Bells jingle as Teddy strolls down the narrow hallway followed closely by Muriel and Toby, who carry several wrapped boxes.

"Merry Christmas!" Muriel greets, a genuinely happy grin filling her face. "I see you've already been out, plowing your driveway." She nods at Jonah with approval.

"Because he's a psycho—oh!" Jonah wraps an arm around my waist and effortlessly lifts me off my feet, earning my squeal.

"I know we're a bit early, but we were just sittin' around, killin' time, so we decided to drive over."

"*She* decided we should drive over. Hope you don't mind," Teddy corrects, shucking his heavy winter coat. Beneath it, he's in head-to-toe red—red button-down shirt, red trousers, red suspenders, red socks.

"You been to the hangar yet today?" Toby asks, feigning indifference.

Jonah chuckles and sets me down. "Yeah, man."

Toby grins. "It's a nice truck! I had a bit of fun, getting that in last night through the snow."

"Here, Calla. This is for you." Muriel thrusts the box she's carrying into my hands before discarding her outer things. "I wore it on my wedding day and it's something you can wear on *your* wedding day. You know, something old *and* something borrowed."

"*Oh.* I …" I eye the box, wariness settling in. By the size of the box, I'm guessing it's not a subtle addition to my wedding attire. I force a smile as I carry it to the dining room table and begin gingerly unwrapping the packaging, a mixture of curiosity and dread swirling inside me. This is a woman who once told me she's happiest wearing her husband's coveralls. She prides herself on *not* caring about such "frivolous things" as clothes.

"You plannin' on reusing that paper? Come on and rip it!" Muriel exclaims, wringing her hands with anticipation.

With a deep breath, I tear a sizeable strip off and lift the box's lid. A mass of fur sits nestled inside tissue paper.

"Now, I know wearing fur is a big taboo these days, but those mink have been dead for almost forty years, so you may as well take 'em out for a walk."

I pull out the stole, its texture luxuriously soft beneath my fingertips.

"And if it makes you feel any better, my father caught 'em tryin' to murder our chickens."

"Oh, Muriel! It's beautiful!" My mother fawns as I drape it over my shoulders. It fits as if custom made for me.

Astrid joins her, stroking the fur. "Look at those colors! Is that a hint of blue I see?"

"Cerulean silver, they called it," Muriel says proudly. "I guess that's your 'something blue,' too? And see the ivory striations?"

There's a chorus of oohs and aahs as I slip it off and hold it up to the light.

"It's gorgeous, Muriel," I admit, a touch of guilt stirring that I doubted her. "I was just saying I needed something like this to go with my dress."

"Well, now you have it. And I know I said 'something borrowed,' but it's yours to keep."

My eyebrows pop with surprise. "Are you sure? I mean, this seems like something you should pass down to family." Her first gun, and now this?

"That's what I'm doin'." She drops an arm around my shoulders to give me an awkward but firm squeeze. "Listen, Deacon's gone, and I've given up on Toby givin' me a daughter-in-law—"

"Are you kidding me?" Toby moans with exasperation. "I'm *only* thirty-five!"

"Yeah, a thirty-five-year-old who's afraid of asking a gal like Emily out to dinner," she retorts before turning her attention back to me. "So, you're it, Calla. You're the closest thing I've got to a daughter. You can wear it for your wedding, and then maybe one day your daughter will wear it to *hers*."

"All *five* of them will wear it," Jonah chirps from next to the fridge while inhaling a bowl of his mother's pudding.

I spare him an eye roll before smiling at Muriel. "Thank you. I love it."

"You're welcome." She pats my shoulder. "Now, have you decided on your menu yet?"

"Not yet—"

"Good, because I have an idea." She turns to my mother. "You didn't seem too keen on the moose, Susan, but how do you feel about grouse?"

"*Grouse?*" my mom echoes, squinting in thought. "That's a bird, right?"

"I love grouse," Björn pipes in from the recliner, busy picking away at a walnut shell he cracked.

"It tastes a bit like partridge," Astrid confirms.

"Well, now, *that* I've had. Remember, Simon, we ordered partridge at that restaurant?" She looks to him for validation.

Simon pauses in his curious inspection of the fur stole to nod fervently. "Yes. I *do*."

Muriel smiles. "Well, good! Because Wendy and John Keating have a game bird farm and they owe me a favor or two. I'm betting I could get as many grouse as you need for next to nothin'. And Gloria makes this recipe, with apples and pecans. I tell ya, I've never had anything like it. She usually serves it with this wild rice pilaf, but it'd be just as good with potatoes, which Calla grew plenty of this past summer."

The ladies pull chairs out around the dining room table and begin reviewing our cellar's inventory from memory, tossing out ideas.

"Muriel's calling in a lot of favors on your behalf," Simon notes quietly.

"She's like the godfather of Trapper's Crossing." All her pushiness and meddling is paying off.

Simon peers at me from over the rim of his glasses. "Any strong opposition to grouse we should be aware of before we let them go too far down this path? Speak up now."

"No. The owner of the lodge made it for us once. It was tasty." If we weren't inviting Andrea and George as guests to our wedding, I would have asked them to cook the meal.

His brow furrows. "So, does it taste like chicken?"

"No. It's gamey." I frown. "You don't remember that partridge dinner Mom was talking about, do you?"

"Not the foggiest clue," Simon admits sheepishly.

CHAPTER ELEVEN

"She pull this kind of shit at home?"

I pause peeling a potato to watch an incensed Jonah hover at the window, his muscular arms folded across his chest, his gaze on the gloomy sky through the windows. The few random flakes sailing down from the sky earlier have multiplied exponentially, sending us toward blizzard territory.

Mabel is almost a full hour late.

"Sometimes," Agnes admits from the sink where she scrubs a pot. "If she's in a mood. She seemed okay today, though."

"I'll tell you right now, things are gonna change when you guys move here in the summer. She won't be trying this with me around."

"Why not? You're around now, and she's not *trying* it, she's *doing* it." Björn studies his cards for a long moment before laying one down on the pile. He, Muriel, Simon, and my mother are playing a game of euchre around the coffee table, while Astrid and Teddy face off at the Swords and Shields board game. We lit several of Phil's old lanterns and positioned them around the main area for added light as the day shifts to night and the power remains out.

Jonah's eyes narrow on his stepfather. They've done a decent job of sidestepping each other since the major blowup two days ago, but I fear that's about to change.

"You forget what you were like at that age, don't you?" Astrid pipes in, likely sensing the impending squabble. "Stubborn, argumentative. You were *always* right."

"So, you're saying I'm about to marry thirteen-year-old Jonah?" I tease, handing Toby the peeled potato to dice and drop into the pot.

My mother guffaws. "You're one to talk. If you weren't screaming at me about how unfair I was for not letting you traipse all over downtown Toronto, you were locked in your room, sulking."

"That's *so* not true!"

"Simon? Would you say that's accurate?"

"I'm going to make it hearts, for my partner," he announces, seemingly missing her question. Or choosing to ignore it.

"Simon—"

"Teenagers need to be kept busy." Muriel shifts the cards around in her hand before laying one on the table. "Deacon and Toby never had time to get into mischief. They were too busy workin' at the resort. Don't you worry. We'll get Mabel occupied with cleanin' cabins and cutting grass, collecting trash. She can even work in the kitchen on busy nights. She'll be so busy makin' money and learning responsibility, she won't have time for mischief. She'll be asleep on her feet at night!"

"And she wonders why I never learned how to talk to women," Toby murmurs under his breath, earning my snort.

"Maybe they're hanging out at the cabin and not getting my messages." Agnes dries her hands on the tea towel. "I think I'll boot over there and see."

"You want me to go?" Jonah offers, taking a step toward the door.

"No, no, you stay put," Agnes is quick to say, heading for her coat and boots. "I could use some fresh air, anyway."

And if Mabel *is* over at the cabin, an angry Jonah blowing up at her won't go over well.

"Last one." I slap the peeled potato into Toby's hand and reach for a homegrown carrot. Muriel was right—yet again. I'm feeling immense satisfaction knowing that everything we're eating today, short of the turkey, was grown in the garden I once despised.

"Oh!" Agnes exclaims at the open door, and for a second I assume it's Mabel, back from her ride, the sound of the snowmobile drowned out by the generator. "It's good to see you, Roy. Calla wasn't sure if you were coming to dinner."

Roy is here?

Roy is actually coming to Christmas dinner?

In the split second of distraction—and shock—I skate the peeler over the corner of my thumb. I drop the carrot with a curse, assessing the stinging damage. It's a tiny wound, though a drop of blood is already forming.

"You're fired." Toby hands me a paper towel and then ushers me away.

"Hey, Jonah. You mind helpin' Roy out?" Agnes hollers.

It's followed by Roy's grumble of, "Don't need help. I got it *in* the truck. I'll get it *out* of the truck."

Jonah spares me a curious glance on his way out.

"Have to say, never thought I'd see the day Roy accepted a dinner invitation," Muriel muses. "What's he up to out there, Teddy?"

Teddy frowns as he cranes his neck to see out the window from his seat. "Can't tell. Whatever it is, it's wrapped in a sheet."

Commotion stirs at the door.

"Christ, Roy. How the hell did you get this into your truck by yourself?" Jonah's muscles strain as he leads with backward steps, holding up one end of the covered object.

"It's awkward, is all." Roy appears on the other end, his feet shuffling along the carpet runner.

I can't help the wide grin of pleasure that takes over my face. He's actually wearing the navy-blue winter coat and wool aviator hat I wrapped and left at his place. They fit him well and they look much warmer than that ratty plaid jacket and raccoon hat.

Roy pauses, his attention wandering over our living room and kitchen, his eyebrows arching as he takes in the festive décor. He stalls on the set dining table before meeting my beaming smile.

His mouth curls at the corners. Only a touch. It's enough for me, though.

"Where should this go, Roy?" Jonah asks.

"Over there." He juts his chin toward the corner next to the fireplace.

"Here. Let me." Jonah stoops to prop what appears to be a beam on his shoulder. With a grunt, he stands, lifting it off the ground.

"My son. The ox," Astrid muses as Jonah carries Roy's surprise delivery across the room. He sets it down with a dull thud.

Roy remains near the door, still in his coat and boots, his hat in his hands, looking as uncomfortable as I've ever seen him.

Agnes has temporarily abandoned her plan to check the cabin for Mabel, sidling up to Roy. "I don't think you've had a chance to meet Astrid and Björn, or Simon yet, have you?" She makes introductions.

"Sounds like you've been taking good care of Calla this year," Simon says by way of greeting.

Roy smirks. "That girl don't need any taking care of. She figures things out fine on her own."

Simon nods, smiling to himself. "I suppose you're right."

"Are we doin' this, Roy?" Jonah is holding Roy's creation upright. It must be what Roy was working on that day I surprised him in his barn.

"Here, let me help you." Muriel marches over to pull the sheet off.

It takes me a moment to recognize it for what it is: a mantel. A stunning, rustic wooden construct in a natural maple stain, with two pillars on either side, meant to frame the hearth.

"Always thought it was silly to have such a big stone fireplace and no mantel," he mutters.

I stumble over a chair leg on my way around the dining table to get a better look. "I was *literally* thinking about this the other day."

"Yeah, well …" Roy shifts on his feet. "I happened to take measurements when I was here in the fall, so I know it'll fit. Should be an easy install whenever you're ready for me to do it."

A prickle of emotion swells in my throat, not because of the thoughtful gift, but because the man who everyone stamped too selfish to think of others was thinking of me. He's proven them wrong, time and time again. "It's perfect. I couldn't have picked a more *perfect* mantel to go here." I smooth a hand over the long cross beam. Where did he get such a large, beautiful piece of wood?

Toby must be thinking along the same lines. "That had to be one hell of a solid wood beam you used for this, huh, Roy?"

"I've had that monster in my shop for years. I was holdin' on to it for the right project."

It suddenly dawns on me. "Was this the beam that fell on you?" That would have crushed him, had the full weight of it not been hindered by other fallen hunks of wood.

Roy shrugs. "Still a good piece of wood."

I shake my head, but I can't help but laugh.

"What?" he challenges, but the way the corner of his mouth curls tells me he sees the twisted humor. Only Roy could make such a lovely gift out of something that nearly killed him.

"This is a nice surprise." Jonah leans the mantel across the stone and then marches over to offer his hand and a solemn, "Thank you, Roy."

Roy accepts it without hesitation.

Oh, how far you've come, curmudgeon. There was a time, not even a year ago, that Roy sneered at that same friendly gesture.

Now, if he'd just come around to reconnecting with his daughter.

I have hope for him yet. It's a matter of me figuring out how to maneuver around that conversation.

First things first, though, I need to speak with Delyla. I responded to her email this morning. I told her, yes, I'd love to talk to her. When, is the issue. Certainly not today. And the next six days will be a madhouse around here, getting ready for the wedding. I need time with her. Time to explain the complexities of a seemingly simple man like Roy Donovan. Time to prepare her for the kindness buried beneath the scowling exterior.

Time to make sure she can't hurt him. I find myself, more than anything, wanting to protect this lonely man who hides from his past, deep in the woods.

"Well ..." He turns and takes a step toward the door.

"Where are you going?" I blurt.

"Home."

"You're not staying for dinner?"

"Nah. I got chores to do. I just came to drop that off." He does another scan of the tree, the table, the half-eaten gingerbread house that's been moved to the kitchen counter. "You folks have yourselves a good night."

Even though I should have expected this, my disappointment surges.

"Glen texted me," Toby calls out, his phone in his hand. "They were expecting Kelly back by now, too, and she's not answering her phone, either."

"Okay. Let me see if they're at the cabin before we sound the alarms." Agnes disappears out the door again.

Roy watches her go. "What's that about, now?"

"Mabel went out for a ride with Glen Prichard's daughter," Toby explains, collecting a carrot to peel. "They should have been home an hour ago and no one can get hold of them."

"Huh." Roy frowns. "Heavy squalls movin' in from the west. Easy to get lost out there in that."

Is he thinking about that night all those years ago, when his mother went out for food in a storm and never came back?

"They're probably over at a friend's house, hangin' out, and lost track of time." But Muriel's furrowed brow says she's not buying that.

Is she thinking about that night all those years ago, when her son stayed out hunting alone and never came back?

Dread crawls up my spine as I begin to appreciate why Jonah's pacing like a caged animal, and how dangerous a situation this might be.

After another beat, Roy walks out the door without a word, in typical Roy fashion.

Five minutes later, Agnes returns, her face lined with worry. "No sign of them there," she confirms.

Jonah curses under his breath. "Okay. I'm gonna go and look for them."

"Toby—" Muriel beckons, but he's already dropping his task and heading for the door.

To Agnes, Jonah promises, "Don't worry. We'll find her. No matter how long it takes."

This is reminding me all too much of that night back in August when I sat in this house, powerless, waiting to hear about Jonah, unable to do anything. I thought I'd lose my mind.

I can't do that again.

"Wait!" I rush for my coat and gloves.

I warm my hands by the fire as I listen to the buzz of voices around me, feeling like a visitor in my own house. Agnes is off to one corner, on the phone with the state troopers, giving as many details about Mabel as she can recall—her height and weight, what she was wearing. Muriel has dug up a map of the area from her glove box and Jonah is marking with a yellow highlighter the trails we spent two hours combing in the blistering-cold wind. Toby is rounding up a small army of friends—all of whom grew up with him and Kelly's father—to congregate by the hangar with their snowmachines in twenty minutes. Teddy is at home, gathering supplies so they can join us in our search.

It's almost six P.M. on Christmas Day. Dinner is getting cold in casserole dishes and on platters. If it were under any other situation, I would feel bad for all Simon's hard work gone to waste. But all I can think about is how dark and frigid it is out there, and how Agnes cannot lose her child to the harsh realities of life in Alaska. She has already lost so much.

"Glen said they probably went north along the river." Toby traces the line on the map with his index finger. "In this weather, even I've gotten turned around a few times up there, and I know that area like the back of my hand."

Björn frowns at the map. "What about west?"

"Nah. They're not allowed to go that way. Too easy to get lost up in there, even in good weather, especially for a bunch of kids."

"Then *that's* the way they went," Björn says matter-of-factly.

Toby's brow furrows. "Kelly's pretty good about sticking to the rules."

"Teenagers don't always do what they're told. I'll bet they went west," Björn presses.

"This isn't a horse race—" Jonah cuts himself off, gritting his teeth to bite back whatever else he's about to say.

"Of course, they could have started north, got twisted up, and ended up goin' west, like those kids a few years ago," Muriel says.

"Remember them? Found them eighteen miles away, frostbitten to hell."

Not helping, Muriel.

"We'll start by following the river north and then fanning out along those trails," Jonah states, sparing Björn nothing more than glare—as if to dare him to counter—before heading over to me. "You gonna stay here?"

"No. I'm going with you."

He shakes his head. "It could be a long night, Calla."

"I don't care." I reach for him, squeezing his hand. "If you're out there all night, then so am I."

He nods. "Okay. But you should add another layer or two."

Björn walks over, his coat and hat in his hands. "What machine can *I* take out?"

Jonah frowns, with surprise or irritation, I can't tell. "There isn't one. We only have the two, and Mabel's got one of them."

"Where can we find another?"

"I don't know, and I don't have time to look for one for you." Definitely irritation.

"What can I do, then?"

"I don't know. Keep the fire burning."

Björn scowls. "But—"

"I don't have time for this." Jonah tugs his hat over his head. "Calla, you got two minutes."

I run up the stairs to find more layers.

Jonah's body is rigid against mine as we sail up the driveway toward the house, and I know it has nothing to do with the chilling cold that has seeped into our bones.

We can't find Mabel or Kelly.

I lost count of the number of people out, riding the trails for hours. But there's not a trace of the girls to be found, the falling snow and blowing wind covering whatever tracks they might have made.

"I hate being on the ground like this. I wish I could use my plane," Jonah snarls, peeling off his helmet.

My heart beats in my throat as we climb the steps, our limbs numb from the ride. The buzz of approaching snowmachines trails behind us. I don't have to look to know it's the McGivneys, who have no intention of leaving us tonight, whether we want them to or not.

This is becoming our routine—tragedy strikes and we congregate. It would be uplifting if not inspired by such horrible events.

Agnes is waiting for us at the door. The grief on her face says she has already received the grim news from the state troopers that they've called off the search until morning due to poor visibility.

"I'm gonna gas up and go back out on my own," Jonah says by way of greeting.

"No, you're not!" we both respond in unison, followed closely by similar reactions from Astrid and my mother.

"You can't go out again tonight. Look at you both. You're frozen!" My mom peels my stiff, snow-caked scarf from around my neck as if to make her point.

"And there are two teenaged girls out there, *frozen*!"

"Jonah!" Astrid scolds.

He smooths a palm over his forehead and tempers his tone. "I'm sorry. But I can't sit around here while she's out there."

"And *I* can't have you *and* Björn going rogue tonight." There's desperation in Astrid's voice.

Jonah's eyes bulge. "What do you mean? Where the hell did Björn go?" He scans our living room, as do I. Only a weary-looking Simon remains, quietly sitting at the dining table by the dim cast of an oil lamp. All the food has been tucked away and the kitchen is spotless.

"He was upset that he was left behind while everyone else went out." Astrid hesitates. "He needs to feel useful in situations like this, and you made him feel old and useless."

Bewilderment mars Jonah's face. "You're kidding me, right? I don't give a shit about Björn's ego right now. You shouldn't, either."

"I'm explaining what happened." Astrid holds a hand up to stall Jonah's rant. "Kelly's mother phoned here to see if we'd heard anything. Björn answered. She mentioned not being able to go look for her daughter because of her two young children at home. So Björn asked if he could borrow her snowmachine to go out and join the search. She agreed to lend it to him."

Jonah looks like his mother slapped him across the face. "Tell me you didn't let a sixty-nine-year-old man from Norway go out into the Alaskan wilderness in a blizzard, *alone*?"

"I tried to stop him," Astrid begins.

"He's not alone. Roy went with him," Agnes says calmly. I don't know how she's keeping her cool at a time like this. "Roy came by about an hour after you guys left. He heard all the engines and thought it might have something to do with Mabel, so he came looking for an update. When he saw how determined Björn was to go out there, he said he'd go with him. Roy drove him over to the Prichards' to get the snowmachine and off they went."

Jonah rubs the back of his neck. "At least he's not *completely* alone."

"He's in good hands if he's with Roy," Muriel says, stepping inside to catch the tail end of the conversation. "He'll make sure they get back."

Astrid offers her an appreciative smile. "They took Mabel's sweater with them. He said Oscar is especially good with scents."

"In this weather?" Jonah runs a hand through his mussed hair. "Not *that* good."

"Actually, I looked it up and research shows wolves can pick up the scent of their prey from two and a half kilometers away, even when it's buried under several feet of snow." Simon frowns. "I mean, not that I think they're—" Clearing his throat, he announces, "I'll boil some water for tea," and scurries off to the kitchen.

"Those two went out *four hours* ago?" Jonah pulls his sleeve up and checks his watch.

"Yes. And it's been at least thirty years since Björn has sat on one of those things. I can't imagine he's too comfortable right now, with his back problems."

"As long as his ego isn't suffering," Jonah mutters dryly.

I bite my tongue against the urge to point out that this all sounds like something Jonah would pull. That's a conversation for later, once everyone's safely home.

"I'm sorry, Mom, but *I've* gotta go back out."

"But what will you possibly be able to see when it's like this?" Astrid pleads.

"I don't know, but there's no way I can sit here with my thumb up my ass while Mabel's out there freezing to death."

"Why don't we take a look at the map to mark off everywhere we've already covered, before we forget." Muriel gestures to the table where it's still laid out. "We'll get a hot tea in us, and then we can all hop out there again, together. Sound good?"

Jonah nods, his brow permanently furrowed.

"I'd like to go out, too," Agnes says, worrying her hands. "I can't sit here anymore—"

"Tell you what, I'll ride with Teddy and you take my machine. Toby, you get started on that map. *I* need a bladder break." She squeezes Agnes's shoulder on her way past—a silent gesture of sympathy to a woman whose child is missing from a woman whose child is forever lost.

Trepidation churns in the pit of my stomach as we set to marking off trail after trail. I knew we'd covered a lot of ground, but I hadn't realized how much.

Twenty minutes later, still frozen to the core, I'm pulling on my bunny boots—a precious Christmas gift from Agnes last year that is saving my feet tonight—when I swear I hear the buzz of an engine. Agnes and Jonah seem to hear it, too, because we all rush for the front porch at once and watch expectantly.

I hold my breath.

Two snowmachines travel up the driveway.

And then another two appear.

It's impossible to tell from this distance who the riders are—if they're searchers coming to check in.

That is until I see two four-legged animals racing beside them.

"It's Roy!" My heart hammers in my chest, desperate for relief. But is it Roy and Björn and volunteers they picked up along the way?

Ten seconds later, Mabel comes to a stop outside our house.

And the dread that's gripped me for hours lifts from my limbs, leaving me feeling weightless.

"Oh, thank God." Agnes pushes out the porch door and runs down the path toward her daughter who has scrambled off the snowmachine. Jonah and I are close behind.

They collide in an embrace, their sobs carrying over the hum of the nearby generator.

"We got lost! No matter where we went, it was the wrong way. It was like we were going in circles. I was so scared! I'm so sorry." Mabel's words tumble from her mouth in a continuous blur.

She towers over Agnes now and yet somehow looks small within Agnes's fierce embrace. "It's okay. You're safe now."

Everyone has filtered out of the house, and a chorus of relieved sighs and exclamations can be heard.

"Oscar found me!" Mabel laughs through her tears. "Can you believe it? Roy said he caught my scent from like a mile away and started running straight toward us."

"Isn't that something." Agnes looks first to the wolf dog, who hangs back, and then to Roy. "Thank you, for finding them and bringing them back."

"Don't thank me." He nods toward Björn. "He's the one who insisted we go west. I didn't think they'd go that way, but he wouldn't let it go. Stubborn pain in my ass."

"I had a gut feeling." Björn struggles to climb off his seat. He says something in Norwegian and Astrid rushes over to take his hand for balance, helping him up. "I forgot what it felt like to sit on one of these for four hours. It's not good."

"Well, look at that. It all worked out." Muriel marches down the path and climbs onto the machine Björn just vacated. "How about I get this back to Noreen for you." She nods at Teddy and Toby, a signal that they should follow suit and swiftly. "Come on, Kelly. Let's get you home, too. I'm sure your parents will be happy to stop worrying."

Kelly turns to Roy to offer him a shy smile. "Thank you."

He grunts in response.

"That's 'you're welcome' in Curmudgeon. He's mastered the language," I explain, earning their giggles and Roy's pointed glare.

"Okay. Let's get you inside." Agnes furiously rubs her daughter's shoulders. "We need to get you checked out by a doctor."

"I think they're gonna be fine. They found an old, abandoned shack and got a decent fire goin'. Stayed huddled. They're smart girls."

"And you're a good man, Roy Donovan!" Muriel hollers over the hum of her engine. "Enjoy the rest of your night!" She takes off, followed closely by Kelly, Toby, and Teddy.

Only Jonah, Roy, and I remain outside in the dark, huddled in our coats and hats, with nothing but the one spotlight fueled by the generator to cast light.

"I'm gonna check on Mabel." Jonah presses a kiss against my cheek and adds reluctantly, "And eat my words for Björn."

I smile. As bullheaded as Jonah can be, when he's wrong, he'll admit it. "Save the really good groveling until I get there. I like watching that."

He snorts. "Good night, Roy. And thanks again." He doesn't wait for Roy's answer before he heads up the path because he knows he won't get one.

I curl my arms around my chest. "Some Christmas Day, huh?" And I thought last year's was memorable.

"You should get on inside. It's gonna take you 'til Friday to warm up."

Speaking of warming up ... "You look good in navy blue." I nod toward his new hat. It's lined with rabbit fur, which I cringed at choosing, but then I wagered that Roy is Roy and isn't likely to wear faux fur. "Maybe Bandit will stop hiding when you come by to see Zeke."

He adjusts his coat sleeve. "It's been awhile since I've had somethin' new to wear."

"And now you have something to wear to our wedding."

He snorts.

"I'm serious, Roy. Please come." I thought more about what my answer *should* have been that night out on the road. "We may not be that important to you, but you're important to us. To *me*. You and Muriel and Toby and Teddy ... you're my family here. If I didn't have you, I'm not sure I'd still be in Alaska. I don't know if Jonah and I would have made it this far." As fiercely as we love each other, sometimes that's not enough.

My parents were proof of that.

I feel my eyes well with emotion. "I'm going to set a place at the table for you, and I *really* hope you're there to fill it. Even if you're in dusty old jeans and that terrible Davy Crockett hat." I back away, not wanting to give him time to formulate another bullshit excuse. "I think we're having grouse for dinner, and I know you hunt them so don't even try to tell me you won't eat that."

I'm halfway up the path when I hear him admit in an oddly

somber tone, "I'm too scared to talk to her."

My feet stall.

"She lost her mother, and the man who raised her. She's lookin' for someone to replace them, and I'm a grumpy old man who'll disappoint her. I've got no love to give anybody. Not her, not her kids." His lips twist. "I don't even remember *how* to love anymore."

"I don't think that's true." I trek back to him. "And I don't think she wants to replace them. She wants to get to know you." I know because I was in her shoes, once.

He studies his worn gloves, and I make a mental note to buy him a new pair of those, too. "Not much to know. I'm a pretty boring guy."

I chuckle. "You're a lot of things, Roy, but boring is *not* one of them."

He shakes his head, still unconvinced. "After what I did to her mother?"

"Maybe she'll ask you about that," I agree. "Maybe she'll want to know why it happened. And maybe knowing that you've regretted it every day since will give her the closure she needs. You won't know until you talk to her. But what I *do* know, from experience, is that it's *never* too late as long as you're both willing to try. And she is, Roy. So have the guts to pick up that phone and call her. Or write her. It'll be the best decision you'll make for the rest of your life." I hesitate. "I can be there when you do that. If you want."

Roy seems to chew on that offer. "You're gonna turn into a Popsicle if you stand out here any longer. Get on inside now, ya hear?" He starts his engine and takes off down the driveway, Oscar and Gus chasing after him.

I smile as I watch him go. "Merry Christmas to you, too."

I'm halfway up the path to the porch when the power comes back on, treating me to a dazzling display of white twinkling lights.

CHAPTER TWELVE

"One more here," my mother says around the bobby pin held between her teeth. She uses it to tuck in a stray hair and then steps back to survey the loose updo we spent the last hour crafting. She smiles, her dazzling, hazel-green eyes drifting the full length of my fitted wedding gown. Connie proved to be a magician, working late into the night, several nights over, pulling apart stitches, snipping excess material, and sewing it back together to tailor fit to my frame. "Perfection."

"Absolute perfection," Diana echoes, stretched out across our bed as if posed for a photo shoot, holding both bouquets. I told her to wear whatever she wants. She chose a sexy Boho chic dress in cranberry that will pop against the frozen backdrop and matches the shade of my mother's dress that Diana brought from home.

"Everything is. Every detail." A lump flares in my throat. "I couldn't have done this without you."

My mom's eyes turn glossy as she collects my hands in hers. "Of course, honey. I've *only* ever wanted this day to be memorable. *For you.*"

I barely notice the pointed lens anymore as Lacey discreetly captures moment after moment, stepping around us almost as if she's not there. She showed me some of her winning shots and there's no doubting her talent. I'm already dying to see the pictures and the day isn't over yet.

The last six days have been a mad flurry of shopping, scavenging, collecting, crafting, and cleaning. We stripped the tackiest of the signs and pictures from the Ale House's walls, tucking them away in boxes for the time being. Surprisingly, my mom wanted to leave the moose and deer heads. They add to the rustic charm, she insisted.

Now they quietly loom over an astonishing transformation that even caught Muriel momentarily speechless when she walked in this morning, to take in the forests' worth of greenery and the lanterns we begged, borrowed, and bought to create ambiance. Toby and Jonah hauled tables over from the community center and lined them up into one long, banquet-style table adorned with rented copper and crystal dishes and ornate candelabras, and every available blush and burgundy flower within a hundred miles of Anchorage. Archie smelled like a florist's cellar when Jonah arrived yesterday with the haul.

"Knock ... knock," Simon calls out from behind the cracked bedroom door. "I've been sent to tell you that they're waiting, and that it's rather cold, so"—he pokes his head in—"if you haven't decided against marrying ..." His words drift, his blue eyes roaming over my dress and face. "Yes, it looks like you're ready to go." An odd, sad smile touches his lips.

"I guess fashionably late doesn't really work when you make people stand beside a frozen lake in Alaska." I reach for the mink stole, my nerves fluttering in my stomach.

With a squeal, Diana shimmies off the bed. "Here, hold these." She thrusts the bouquets into Simon's hands, freeing hers up to slide on the ivory fur stole I gifted her.

Simon leans in to inhale the fragrant roses and eucalyptus leaves while he waits silently, a distinguished gentleman in his staple three-piece gray herringbone tweed suit, another procurement from home, thanks to Diana.

"Thank you." She scoops them from his grip, leaning in to plant a kiss on his cheek before sashaying out. "I'll be downstairs!"

"One more trip to the powder room for me," my mom announces, sweeping past Simon with a pat against his arm.

"Would you mind giving us a moment, please?" he asks Lacey.

With a smile, the willowy blonde ducks out, grabbing her beanie from the dresser on the way.

"Any last grand words of wisdom?"

Simon sucks in a deep breath. "The powder room is code. Your mother is pulling the car around back as we speak. There's still time to make a run for it."

I burst out with laughter. "I'm not going anywhere. I'm not going to change my mind."

"Well then …" He fusses with the caramel-colored buttons on his vest for a moment. "I know I'm not your cool and wild, bush plane–flying dad, but if you don't mind"—he clears his throat, and when he speaks again, that British lilt is gruff—"I'd like to take you down there to get married now."

Tears that I've managed to keep at bay stream freely now. I miss my father with every fiber of my being. I wish I could hear his soft chuckle again. I wish I could watch him climb out of his beloved planes. I wish he were here to see Jonah and me get married. I know it was what he would have wanted.

And if he were alive? He'd be walking me down the aisle.

He'd be on my right side, while Simon walked on my left. "You're right. You're *not* my cool, plane-flying dad." I reach up to adjust his tie, an exact match to the cranberry of my mother's dress. "You're my wise and patient and dependable dad who will *never* play second fiddle to anyone. Not even Wren Fletcher."

He swallows, his own eyes misting. "I suppose that's pretty cool, too."

I giggle, dabbing at my tears with my fingertips. "Yeah, it is."

With another deep breath to gather his composure, he offers me his elbow. "Are we going to do this?"

I smile. "We are."

Michael begins strumming his guitar as soon as Diana rounds the corner of the house. It's followed closely by Ann's melodic twang.

"Oh, they're *good*," Simon murmurs, holding me tight as we pick our way down the cleared path, lined with evergreen-filled urns. "*Really* good."

"Yeah. Thank God," I whisper back, another box to check off, another relief. They were away this past Sunday, so I couldn't even go to church with Muriel to listen to them perform.

"I don't know if I've ever heard this song. It's lovely."

"It is." Twinges of nostalgia stir in my heart. I first heard it while watching *Notting Hill* with my father. We must have watched that movie—and every Julia Roberts movie in his collection—a half dozen times in those last weeks.

My stomach flips with nervous excitement as we clear the crop of birch trees. A huddled group of beaming familiar faces greets us, and I try to take them all in, each in turn. Everyone who was invited is here. Bobbie and George got the message on their phone while in town for supplies and flew back early from vacation at their remote cabin. Andrea and Chris entrusted the lodge's New Year's Eve crowd to their manager. Two of the fire boss crew that Jonah fought fires with this summer flew home from their contract jobs in California just for this.

Everyone came.

Even Roy.

He's standing off to the side, away from everyone, his wide-brimmed cowboy hat hiding his eyes from me. He looks ready to bolt before the ceremony is over.

But he came.

Having greeted everyone with at least a glance, I finally turn my attention to Jonah, my handsome and steadfast pillar in a three-piece charcoal twill suit standing at the end of the lengthy red carpet, the sun an hour from setting above him. Archie sits behind him, waiting to take us on our first flight as husband and wife, an insistence of Jonah's that I couldn't refuse. Teddy stands next to him on the left, beaming and ready to officiate, and a polished Marie in a dazzling black dress to act as best woman stands on his right.

The intensity in Jonah's icy-blue eyes as he watches me approach makes my heart stutter and then pound as strongly now as it did in those hours, days, weeks of first looks, first touches, first kisses. Only now that reaction is roused by something far deeper than a ruggedly handsome face and pretty eyes.

Now, it's Jonah's fearless confidence that makes my blood race.

His unwavering loyalty that makes me search for him in every room.

His untamed passion that makes me weak at the knees.

It's everything—inside and out, good and bad—that makes up this wild man's heart.

And he's about to become mine till death do us part.

Jonah leaves his spot, moving swiftly toward me.

Marie is fast, though, grabbing his arm. "No! Remember? You need to wait for her!" she scolds through a chuckle. The small crowd behind us joins in with laughter.

His jaw tenses and he mouths, "Hurry up."

I sigh as I leave the snow-covered ground and take my first step on the carpet.

"You seem relieved," Simon muses. "Were you actually afraid he wouldn't show?"

"No. But I *was* afraid he was going to wear one of those herre-bunad things." Traditional Norwegian garb with pants that look an awful lot like lederhosen, in my opinion. I'm not sure even Jonah could pull off that look. "He's up to *something*. I know it."

"Ah, yes." Simon's brow furrows. "I'm not entirely certain, but I'm a tad concerned it might have to do with that raccoon. And your ring."

EPILOGUE

July

"There was this *huge* field full of them, so Jonah decided to just *land* right there. I don't know if I'll *ever* get used to him doing that." I chuckle as I tuck the bouquet of vibrant purple wildflowers into the mason jar of water and then set it next to the white cross. "Sure was beautiful, though."

The cemetery is oddly quiet for such a balmy summer day. I drove through Bangor on my way here, and it was bustling, people trudging along the dusty roads, carrying bags of groceries and greeting neighbors. The parking lot at Meyer's was crammed. Agnes said the store shelves were bare all week after a lengthy storm system lingered, grounding cargo planes for days. I guess they must have restocked.

I adjust the small model plane, shifting it to sit closer to the flowers. "Agnes and Mabel are flying home with us today. You should see their new place." The construction company we hired to build the prefab log house told us it wouldn't take long to erect the building once the ground was level. They weren't lying. One week there was flat ground by the lake's edge where trees had been. The next? A small but beautiful two-story home. A parade of tradesmen have cycled through since, installing electrical and plumbing, flooring and kitchen cabinetry.

Now it's Roy's turn for all the final touches. He's far from finished, but Agnes is anxious to get settled, her house in Bangor sold and emptied of personality. She also said she doesn't mind the curmudgeon milling about with his chisel and saw, not saying much. For his part, he doesn't seem to mind her chattering.

"The garden is growing *wild*. I must have made a thousand jars of strawberry jam. I mean, it was realistically more like fifty, but it *felt* like a thousand. And there's this zucchini that's already three times the size of all the other zucchini. It's a mutant. Muriel says we should enter it in some giant vegetable competition when it's full grown. But, I'll probably sell it at the farmers' market." I trace the letters that spell out my father's name. They could probably use a fresh coat of paint soon. "Delyla's coming. Did I tell you that already? I can't remember if I did. She's flying up with her kids next week. They're going to stay with us." The day after Christmas, I woke up and called her. Before coffee, still in bed. I didn't wait. I didn't waffle. I called and she answered on the third ring, her sweet southern twang carrying surprise through the phone line.

I told her all about the Roy Donovan that *I* know, the one who is always there for a neighbor in need, who may not choose the right words but somehow always ends up letting you know how he *really* feels. The man that I've come to care for as deeply as if he were my own family.

The man who is far more than he seems, and whose regrets are bottomless.

We talked for over an hour, until my mother came in, tapping her watch impatiently.

Delyla thanked me and asked if she could call me sometime in the future.

She called the next week.

The week after that, I emailed her a few candid shots of Roy from our wedding. She thanked me profusely.

And the next week, she emailed a letter for Roy that she asked me to print out and give to him. I left it on his kitchen table. He grumbled and snarled for three days, dubbing me Muriel Junior. And then he showed up at our house out of the blue, asking me to teach him how to use one of those goddamn computers. So I set him up with an account and left him alone to type out his thoughts. It took him three hours to finish that first email and hit Send. Delyla confided in me that it was only seven sentences long and riddled with apologies.

After that, Roy started showing up at our house every Monday like clockwork, with handwritten drafts of what he wants to say to his daughter. I leave him be in the office. He's sometimes in there for hours, cursing at the keyboard, his two-fingered typing painfully slow.

In April, I set up a video call for the two of them. He barely said two words. He seemed dumbstruck. It didn't matter because Delyla likes to talk. For a while, I was worried he'd complain about his ear falling off, but he didn't. He's improved his video-calling skills since then, asking questions and answering them with complete sentences. I've even caught him with that rare smile, which doesn't seem to be quite so rare anymore, especially when Gavin and Lauren are present.

I've found a kinship with Delyla, either because of our connection to Roy or my own estrangement with my father. We've forged a friendship of our own over the long winter months, sometimes spending hours on FaceTime, laughing and chatting about nothing and everything.

When she suggested coming up to Alaska, I didn't hesitate to offer her a place to stay. It took me three days to work up the nerve to tell Roy that his daughter was coming here to meet him face-to-face. He was annoyed at first, but he didn't damn me to hell for meddling.

I'd say the curmudgeon is definitely coming around.

I check my phone. "Jonah should be back from flying Marie to the villages." She came to our house in a huff the other day, begging to tag along on this trip to Bangor. She said she needed to get away "from it all." I'm not sure what "it all" is, but I'm guessing it has to do with a certain sled dog breeder that Toby said she's feuding with.

I study the simple solemn cross, still remembering the day it was placed. An ache stirs in my chest. "Why does it feel like we're leaving you behind?" Like the last ties to Western Alaska are being cut. With Agnes and Mabel in Trapper's Crossing, there's no real reason to come this way anymore. "I guess that's not really possible, though, is it? You're still everywhere to me." When I hear the buzz of a plane overhead, I like to think it's Wren Fletcher, doing what he loves most, flying high over the mountains, over the land he loved so deeply. He just doesn't need to land anymore.

"Hey, Calla!" Jonah's deep voice carries from the edge of the cemetery. I didn't hear him pull up. "Sorry, but are you about done there? 'Cause there's some weather comin' in that I'd like to get ahead of. Aggie's all packed."

I see him leaning against George's borrowed truck, his USAF ball cap pulled low on his brow, a soft, black cotton T-shirt clinging to his powerful frame. He'll wait for me out there. He never intrudes on my time at my dad's grave.

"I don't know when I'll be back here again." I bite my lip as my stomach erupts in a wild rush of butterflies. "But can I let you in on a little secret? One I haven't even told Jonah yet?"

I lean in.

And I whisper the words that are about to make my husband very happy.

Catch up with Calla, Jonah, and the rest of
Trapper's Crossing, Alaska in
Dr. Marie Lehr's story.

Title and release date to come.

THE PLAYER NEXT DOOR - SNEAK PEEK

Chapter One

2007

I survived Day One without puking or crying.

Do they make T-shirts with that slogan? They must. I can't be the only person to head back to school after summer vacation with a broken heart. Though, I'd be lying if I wore that T-shirt. I *did* cry today; I just didn't do it in public. I ducked into a restroom stall as the first fat tear rolled down my cheek and then spent my entire lunch period with my butt planted on a toilet seat, struggling to muffle my sobs as giggling girls streamed in and out, oblivious.

And all it took was one look from Shane Beckett to cause that reaction. Or rather, the lack of a look. A passing glance as we crossed paths in the hallway between third and fourth period, when his beautiful whiskey-colored eyes touched mine before flickering away, as if the momentary connection was accidental.

As if the seventeen-year-old, six-foot star quarterback for the Polson Falls Panthers and I hadn't spent the summer in a semi-permanent lip-lock.

As if last night, sitting in his father's car outside my apartment building, he didn't tell me that we were getting too serious, too fast, and he couldn't handle a relationship right now, that he needed to focus on football, and I was too much of a distraction.

That one vacant, meaningless look from Shane Beckett in the hall today was worse than anything else he could have done, and it sent me stumbling away, dragging my obliterated spirit behind me.

The rest of the day has been a painful blur, with me cowering in the same restroom stall after the last bell rang to avoid the crowd. I foresee myself spending a lot of time in there. Maybe I should hang an occupied sign and declare it mine for the school year.

"Hey, Scarlet." Becca Thompson, her stride buoyant, flashes a sympathetic smile as she passes me on the steps outside the front doors of Polson Falls High.

"Hey," I manage, but the bubbly blond is already gone, trotting down the sidewalk, no glance backward, almost as if she hadn't greeted me at all. She's nice enough, but I shouldn't be surprised by the lukewarm friendliness. We've never traveled in the same circles, her being the popular cheerleader and me being the reticent mathlete who slogs away at the local drive-in movie theater every weekend in summer. We'd exchanged nothing more than polite greetings before Shane and I started dating, despite our mothers working together at the hair salon for years.

Couple that with the fact that Becca is best friends with Penelope Rhodes—a.k.a. the Red Devil, otherwise known as the worst human to walk these dank halls—who was away in Italy all summer, and I'm not surprised that I'm persona non grata once again.

Becca obviously knows Shane and I broke up. They *all* must know. But at least she acknowledged me, so I guess there's that.

She's heading toward the parking lot now. That's where the jocks and cheerleaders and otherwise popular crowd hang out, congregated around the cars their parents bought for them, talking and laughing and ignoring the peasants.

I check my watch. It's been twenty minutes since the last bell. Most of them *should* have left by now. With a heavy sigh, I tuck a wayward strand of my mouse-brown bob behind my ear, hike my backpack over my shoulder, and amble down the path, ready to avoid eye contact and walk the eight blocks home where I can hide in my bedroom for the rest of my life—or at least for the night.

Rounding the bend, I spot Steve Dip heading this way with two other guys from the football team. My stomach clenches. There's a reason the wide receiver and Shane's best friend is nicknamed Dipshit. He's an obnoxious ass with a cruel sense of humor.

I hold my breath, hoping he'll ignore me, like everyone else seems to be.

Our eyes meet and he winks. *No such luck*. "Hey, BB. You cost me fifty bucks!"

I frown. *What?* I have no idea why he's calling me that, but it can't mean anything flattering, especially not with the raucous laughter that follows.

He brushes a hand through his cropped hair. "Tell Dottie I'm gonna come in for a *quickie* later, will ya?"

"Bite me," I throw back, my cheeks burning as we pass. How long has he been sitting on that stupid joke? It's far from the first time I've heard something along those lines. When your mother's the town bicycle, everyone feels the need to share their punch line with you. He never dared say a word about her when Shane and I were together, but I guess it's no holds barred now.

"Is that an offer?" Steve grins. "'Cause it sounds like that'd be more action than Bex got this summer."

I lift my middle finger in the air and speed up, wanting to put as much distance as possible before this knot in my throat explodes into tears. I told Shane I wanted to take it slow and he said that was fine. He never pushed me.

Did he tell his friends? Was he laughing about it with them? Mocking me?

The parking lot has emptied out with only a few students lingering. Aside from Dean Fanshaw, no one left is associated with Shane and that crowd. Thank God.

Dean is Shane's very best friend and, unlike Steve, isn't known for being a jerk. What he *is* known for—and for good reason, based on what I witnessed—is boning every girl who's willing. Currently, he's too busy mauling Virginia Grafton's neck against the hood of his truck to notice me.

I keep my eyes forward as I rush past them and his red pickup, trying my best not to think about warm summer nights stretched out in the back of it, cradled between Shane's long, muscular thighs, my back resting against his chest, struggling to focus on the movie playing on the drive-in screen ahead.

I'm so focused on *not* catching Dean's attention that I almost miss the two sets of legs dangling over the open tailgate, tangled in each other.

Almost.

One set, long and male, I recognize instantly. It's the shoes I recognize, actually—white Vans. Shane's favorite.

The other legs are shapely and lead into a short, powder-pink skirt that I distinctly remember from second period English.

I'm frozen in place as I watch Shane and Penelope Rhodes lost in a kiss, Shane's fingers woven through her fiery-red hair, while his other hand slips beneath that tiny skirt.

I was *so* wrong.

Ignoring me earlier was *not* the worst thing Shane Beckett could have done today.

Chapter Two

August 2020

I inhale the stale air in the living room, rife with the smell of old wood steeped in summer's humidity. The widow Iris Rutshack left the house spotless, at least. Or rather, her children must have, because I can't imagine the ninety-year-old woman on her hands and knees, scrubbing grime off the thick pine baseboards.

I smile with giddiness.

This place is *mine*.

I used to walk past this charming clapboard house every day on my way home from school. I'd admire the pale blue exterior and the covered porch running along the front, adorned by a matching set of rocking chairs that Mr. and Mrs. Rutshack—old even back then—filled every afternoon, watching the kids go by. On the odd day that their watchful gazes were distracted by a singing bird at their feeder, I'd stick my hand between the fence pickets and steal a bloom from the wild English-style garden that bordered the sidewalk.

Then I'd keep going all the way home to our low-rent apartment complex, my feet growing heavier with each step closer. When I closed my eyes at night, I'd imagine I was drifting off to the rhythmic sound of creaking chairs and cricket chirps, and not to the barfly screwing my mom on the other side of a too-thin wall.

"Thanks, Gramps. Whoever you are." My voice echoes through the hollow space as I wander. Technically, my father's father bought the house for me. He was never a part of my life, but he knew who I was—the product of a fling between his twenty-eight-year-old, truck-driver son with a criminal record and my then-fifteen-year-old mother—and was kind enough to name me in his will.

The house needs some TLC, more evident now that the furniture is gone. Nothing fresh paint, new lights, and a belt sander to the worn golden oak floors can't fix. I knew that when I put an offer in, and ever since I signed the sale papers, my butt's been glued to the shabby couch of my Newark apartment while I've binge-watched home-reno shows for inspiration. Of course, most of it I can't afford. Slowly but surely, though, I'll turn this place into the charming seaside retreat—minus the sea—that I've always envisioned.

Checking the time, I fire off a quick "Where are you?" text to my best friend, Justine, and then head to the porch to wait for the U-Haul. They were supposed to be here an hour ago. I'm annoyed, but I can't be too annoyed, seeing as Joe and Bill—Justine's brother and boyfriend—are driving two hours each way to move me in exchange for beer and burgers and a night on air mattresses.

Well, I'm sure Justine will repay Bill in some sordid way that I'd rather not think about.

Leaning against the post, I smile at the hum of a lawn mower churning through grass in the neighborhood. I'll have to pay a neighborhood boy to cut my front yard until I can afford my own mower. The gardens, I'll tend on my own. Iris and her husband doted on this property for sixty years, and I promised her I'd keep them thriving. Maybe that's a tall order, seeing as I have yet to keep even a cactus alive. First stop tomorrow is to replace my long-lost library card so I can borrow some gardening books.

The low picket fence—more decorative than purposeful—that lines the front yard has seen better days, the layers of white paint peeling away, many of the boards needing new nails to secure them upright. The wooden rocking chairs will need attention too. They rest where they always have. Iris left them, saying they belong on this porch. I can't bring myself to sit in one just yet, so I settle on the slanted porch steps instead.

Two children coast along the quiet, oak-lined street on their bicycles, throwing a curious glance my way. I'm sure they saw the For Sale sign out on the curb weeks ago. In a town this small, everyone is interested to know more about the woman moving into the neighborhood.

They don't have to worry about me, though. I'm a native of Polson Falls, Pennsylvania, merely displaced for twelve years when I dashed away to college in New York, allured by the idea of starting over in a big city where people hadn't heard the names Scarlet or Dottie Reed. It was fun for a time, but I've since learned big cities aren't all they're cracked up to be, and the luxury of anonymity has its own set of challenges. Like, how hard it is to catch a break in a school board where you have no connections. Seven years of substitute teaching while waitressing in the evenings to make ends meet dulled the luster for that life.

It seemed like providence then, when I made the obligatory trip home to visit Mom for her birthday and ran into my elementary school principal at the 7-Eleven. Wendy Redwood always loved me as a student. We got to talking about my teaching career. Thirty minutes of chatter and what felt like an impromptu interview later, she asked me if I'd ever consider working for her. Lo and behold, she's *still* the principal at Polson Falls Elementary and was looking for a sixth grade teacher for the fall. Sure, there were hiring considerations and board rules and all that, but she could navigate around them. Wink, wink. Nudge, nudge.

I smiled and thanked her and told her I'd think about it. At the time, I couldn't imagine entertaining the thought, but then I drove down Hickory Street for shits and giggles, only to see the open-house sign in front of my childhood dream home.

Within fifteen minutes of stepping inside, I was dialing Wendy Redwood for the job and considering what I should offer on the property. It all seemed like kismet. I mean, the house was at a price almost too good to be true, and the school was two blocks away!

I sigh as I sip the last of my cold, burnt gas station coffee. This is a fresh start, even in an old world full of familiar faces. Besides, it's been more than a decade since I last roamed the halls of any school here. Those painful years and cruel people are far behind me.

The peaceful midday calm is disrupted by the chug of a garage door crawling open, followed by the deep rumble of a car engine starting. A long, red vintage muscle car backs out of the garage next door and eases into the open space beside a blue Ford pickup. I can't tell what kind of car it is, but it's old and in pristine shape, the bright coat of paint glistening in the August sun.

I never asked Iris about the neighbors. The two times I've been here—once during the open house and once after I'd signed the paperwork for the offer—nobody was home on either side. Both properties look well maintained, though. The bungalow with the muscle car has new windows and a freshly built porch off the front. There isn't much in the way of gardens—some shrubs and trees—but the lawn is manicured.

I watch curiously as the driver's side door pops open and a tall man with wavy, chestnut-brown hair steps out, his back to me as he fusses with his windshield wiper. Coffee pools in my mouth as I stall on my swallow, too busy appreciating the way his black T-shirt clings to his body, showing off broad, sculpted shoulders, muscular arms, and a tapered waist. He's wearing his dark-wash jeans perfectly—not so baggy that they hang unflatteringly off his ass, but not so tight that cowboy boots and a wide-brimmed hat come to mind.

Damn.

I hold my breath in anticipation, hoping my neighbor will show me a beautiful face to match that fitness-model body. What a stroke of luck that would be, to live next to a gorgeous man. A *single*, gorgeous man, I pray.

Finally, my silent pleading is answered as he turns and his gaze drifts my way.

I struggle not to spew coffee from my mouth as my keen interest turns to horror.

Oh my God.

Someone, please tell me this is a mistake.

Please tell me I'm not living next door to Shane Fucking Beckett.

Read The Player Next Door now!

katuckerbooks.com/theplayernextdoor

ACKNOWLEDGMENTS

I hope you've enjoyed a bit more time with Calla and Jonah in this holiday novella. While I would love to hang out with them forever, it's time to move on. The Simple Wild world has grown beyond these two, to a full cast of dynamic characters. One in particular deserves her own happy ending. I mean, unrequited love where the object of her desire is her best friend, the yeti? Talk about heartbreaking. It's also good fodder for a new story. I can't wait to write it, and I hope you'll read it.

I'd like to take a minute to say an enormous thank you to my readers. You continue to shout about this series to anyone who will listen, and I continue to receive pleasant messages from new readers, excited to have discovered these characters and my books in general. You guys keep shouting and I will keep writing, deal?

I'd like to thank the following people for their help pulling this book together:

Linda Marie Drage, my Norwegian checkpoint.

Amber Sloan, for answering my random questions about Alaska.

Jenn Sommersby, for editing this darling ... for your darling.

Chanpreet Singh, for sliding me into your schedule and catching those pesky last little errors.

Hang Le, for your cover-witch magic.

Nina Grinstead and the team at Valentine PR, for spreading the word about this book release.

Stacey Donaghy of Donaghy Literary Group, for being my sounding board and my support.

Tami, Sarah, and Amélie, for helping to maintain a positive and drama-free reader group—the only place on Facebook I enjoy being nowadays.

My family, just because.

ABOUT THE AUTHOR

K.A. Tucker writes captivating stories with an edge. She is the internationally bestselling author of the Ten Tiny Breaths and Burying Water series, He Will Be My Ruin, Until It Fades, Keep Her Safe, The Simple Wild, Be the Girl, and Say You Still Love Me. Her books have been featured in national publications including USA Today, Globe & Mail, Suspense Magazine, Publisher's Weekly, Oprah Mag, and First for Women. She has been nominated for the Goodreads Choice Award for Best Romance 2013 for TEN TINY BREATHS and Best Romance 2018 for THE SIMPLE WILD. KEEP HER SAFE made Suspense Magazine's Best of 2018 list for Romantic Suspense.

K.A. Tucker currently resides in a quaint town outside of Toronto.

Learn more about K.A. Tucker and her books at katuckerbook-s.com and sign up for her occasional newsletter.

Printed in Great Britain
by Amazon

37302483R00091